GIRL
ZOO

GIRL
ZOO

AIMEE PARKISON
AND CAROL GUESS

TUSCALOOSA

Inquiries about reproducing material from this work should be addressed
to The University of Alabama Press

Book Design: Publications Unit, Department of English, Illinois State
    University; Director: Steve Halle, Production Intern: Megan Donnan
Cover Design: Lou Robinson
Typeface: Baskerville

Library of Congress Cataloging-in-Publication Data

Names: Parkison, Aimee, 1976- author. | Guess, Carol, 1968- author.
Title: Girl zoo / Aimee Parkison and Carol Guess.
Description: Tuscaloosa, Alabama : The University of Alabama Press,
[2019] |
  Includes index.
Identifiers: LCCN 2018041875 (print) | LCCN 2018045913 (ebook) |
ISBN
  9781573668828 (E-Book) | ISBN 9781573660709 (pbk.)
Classification: LCC PS3616.A7545 (ebook) | LCC PS3616.A7545 A6
2019 (print) |
  DDC 813/.6—dc23
LC record available at https://lccn.loc.gov/2018041875

CONTENTS

ONE

GIRL IN CLOCK

THE GIRL IN THE CLOCK learned how to tell time before we did. It felt like cheating to spin her around.

"Six," I said, and gave her a twirl. She moaned, arms stretched as far as they'd go.

"Twelve," Leah said.

"That's nothing. That's just her standing still with her arms in the air."

"But she'll get tired and her arms will hurt."

"Twelve's not even a stretch. At least try three."

The clock was on Mr. Baxter's desk. We could hear her trapped inside.

"She's grunting."

"Is she, though?" I shuffled through the stack of papers on his desk. "I can't hear anything. Let's try four."

"AM or PM?"

"We've been through this, Leah. There's no way to tell. The clock is just round and the numbers don't change."

"Then how did people know what time it was? In the old days. With clocks. Before cell phones and drones."

"Maybe they didn't. Maybe some people hung out during the day and slept at night, and some people hung out at night and slept during the day, and they never realized it."

"Like, two separate worlds. Until one day this woman couldn't sleep and saw people surfing in the middle of the night."

"To her."

"Huh?"

"The middle of the night to her. But it was daytime to them."

"But it was dark."

"But if it was their daytime, they wouldn't care." I rummaged through Mr. Baxter's coat pockets. "Want some gum?"

"Daisy, you can't play with the teacher's stuff. That's why we're always in trouble."

"We're always in trouble because you always get caught."

"What are you going to tell him when he looks for his gum?"

"People who chew gum always have a secret pack."

"A secret pact with who?"

"Not pact. Pack. Like, pack of gum."

"But he's still going to … "

"Listen." The girl in the clock was at it again. Groaning, moaning, arms stretched wide. "She's inside with all the spinning numbers." I pressed the clock to my ear. "She's screaming, Leah. If we don't set her free she'll die, and blood will drip from the clock, and we'll feel terrible and go to hell and we won't be able to text anymore."

"Blood. Gross."

"You eat meat, don't you?"

"Meat doesn't have blood."

"Meat is blood, Leah."

"I hate when you make me feel stupid."

"Should we let Mr. Baxter out of the closet?"

Leah shrugged. "I guess. But will he do it again?"

"If he does it again, I'll put him back. I just think maybe he needs some air."

"I don't think he does." Leah scratched an itch on her ankle. "My socks are prickly. I hate wool socks."

"What if he can't breathe? I mean, we tied his mouth up pretty tight."

"His hands, too."

"Should we check?"

"No." Leah took off her shoes and socks and scratched her ankles feverishly. "I'm sure he's fine. He can breathe through his nose."

We started to listen to the sound behind the closet door. We didn't mean to hurt him, but he had been playing with the girl in the clock. That was his mistake.

"Hey," Leah whispered, chewing gum like cud. "What's that?"

"More blood! Where's it coming from?"

I wondered, should we free the girl in the clock or Mr. Baxter?

Being trapped in the clock, she was free from time and could make herself into a baby, a young woman, a girl, a crone, or even an embryo.

As an embryo, she entered men's heads and had already gone inside Mr. Baxter once, but rocketed out when he sneezed while chewing gum. A learned man rescued by mucus, saved by snot, boogers were his salvation. She usually chose the nose, traveling straight to the brain, but Mr. Baxter's habit of sneezing excessively near the clock saved his life.

I pointed at snot splattered beside the ashtray of chewed gum shaped like a python.

"Gag," Leah said.

Since the girl in the clock was often trapped and as cute as a button, men thought it was safe to steal her. Being an embryo, she could wiggle into noses and blow heads apart as she grew inside a skull, often emerging fully formed like Athena from Zeus. An infant, a child, an old woman retreating into embryo: if only men could be like Zeus, their heads could handle giving birth to her.

I have been overjoyed near exploding heads as she grows inside bloody brains like a migraine when men have no idea what's happening. Right before our eyes! In a matter of minutes, we can watch her mature.

We've seen so many exploding heads and love watching her burst a baby through a man's brain.

I like to catch her sliding through an exploding head, hands slick with blood as she giggles, gulping air.

God, I love her!

I've never loved anyone the way I love her.

Even if she's evil, she's my baby.

Even if she's a serial killer, she's my sister.

Even if she lusts for blood, she's my mother.

Even if she rapes men's noses, she's my mentor, my timeless grandmother baptizing me in gore.

Though I fear she might go inside me, I need to hold her close, to watch as she goes from being my baby to my sister to my mother to my grandmother and back into the clock to sleep.

The clock is dripping blood. We must free her, or she will die. I can't wait to see her again, but poor Mr. Baxter!

GIRL IN DOG HOUSE

Dad lives in Green Meadow Terrace Estates. When he moved out of the yellow house he promised I could have a cat, and when I live with him, I do. I have a hundred cats in the walls of his apartment. It smells like cheese and orange juice.

Mom lives in the yellow house, hoarding dogs. Strange kennels appear everywhere and I don't know where they're coming from. The walls have massive holes full of puppies. We crawl around the house with a flashlight gazing into puppy holes. We have to throw dog food inside the holes in the walls.

When he first moved to Terrace, Dad was all about the ladies. Old school hookups, one shot at a time. First Nancy, then Mona, then Rae, then Tamika. Now it's Sadie, and she sees the cats too.

"We're in this together," she says. I don't know if she means Dad or the cats. Sadie is my pick, and Dad says that's good because she's his pick, too. At school, families are all different and the teachers aren't allowed to say one kind of family is better than another, but they do anyway. We aren't allowed to have guns, but sometimes we shoot.

Mom has a gun and Dad has a gun. Sadie has a toothbrush that vibrates; there's a battery inside. "But will the battery get wet?" I ask, thinking of guns in the walls of the house.

Dad has a gun safe. The combination is 1–2–3–4. Mom has a box under her bed and it locks with a key taped to the top.

I know how to shoot because Sadie taught me. She said hold onto your toothbrush and don't let go. Pointing it at her head she said shoot to kill. She said head or heart. She said if you miss, you'll shoot something else.

Out in the woods behind the yellow house.

Down by the river near Dad's apartment.

Between boxcars by the port where I ride my bike.

Straddling the train tracks where kids go to smoke.

These are my practice places, my kickbacks. I take Mom's gun when I go to Dad's and I take Dad's gun when I go to Mom's. They don't notice anything. They have other guns, other kids from other lives. They have books on tape and barbecue sauce.

Mom's boyfriend Luke makes soundtracks for commercials. Like that commercial for auto insurance where the whole family dies except the sister, left behind in the rest stop, still combing her hair.

I have a gun and I have bullets and I'm teaching myself to aim for the heart.

Out in the woods behind the yellow house I shoot leaves from trees.

Down by the river near Dad's apartment I shoot cans on a log.

Between boxcars by the port where I ride my bike I don't shoot anything.

Straddling the train tracks where kids go to smoke I name all the names and the mean girls go down. One by one, blood on the tracks. My make-believe movie; in real life, they just laugh.

We don't have metal detectors at school. We have signs that say *No Drugs No Guns*. We have signs that say *Dirty Hands Spread Disease*. We spend hours on dead names and hours on kickball. We kick and we kick but our teachers can't text, can't navigate the internet. They want to be our friends on Facebook. They want us to teach them what it means to live now.

After school, I walk to Mom's. The walls of the yellow house howl around me. When I close my eyes, I'm surrounded by puppies. I feel their warm fur, smell the meat on their breath.

Sometimes Sadie and I watch shows while Dad's working late, or whatever he calls it. Dad doesn't deserve her, but maybe I do. We binge watch the bloodiest shows on TV.

Sometimes Dad stays out all night. Sadie and I sleep head to toe on the sofa. We name all the cats, working backwards from Z. We sleep soundly in Kevlar, guns safe in our holes.

GIRL IN MANSION

PERCHED ON TOP OF A HILL, the 21,000-square-foot, four story home with thirty-two entrances has so many twists, turns, and corridors that the girl gets lost for days, crying inside expansive rooms, moving from fireplace to fireplace while eating dust bunnies, insects, and leaves from windowsills. Because the house has fifty-five rooms, thirty-eight beds, and twelve bathrooms, seven televisions are far too few.

She knows she will never get out when the mansion's owner tells her to tie a string to her wrist so she can find her way back to the living room. Night and day, she walks, attached to a giant ball of string, unspooling.

"Where am I?" she asks.

The mansion's owner tells her to talk to the architect's grandson, also an architect, like his father before him.

"Well, for one thing," the architect says, "you're in a starter mansion."

"What?" she asks.

"Never mind," says the owner. "Just pay attention to what the architect says."

"This home was built in 1911 of bricks divided by hand-hewn timbers," says the architect, "the mortar squashed out when the bricks were laid and wasn't wiped."

10

"Remember this," says the owner.

"This method of not wiping the oozing mortar and letting the ooze dry for dramatic effect," says the architect, "is called 'waterfall mortar.'"

"Waterfall mortar," she whispers, liking the sound of those words.

"Think on it, girl," the owner says with a smile as he lights a Cuban cigar. "How could a secretion, emission, excretion, something that is basically a white discharge from bricks, create something as beautiful and poetic as a permanent waterfall on walls?"

"Amazing," she whispers, trying to appreciate it because she is just starting to understand she is a part of it now.

Later, she realizes the entire mansion is this way, its designers having found ways to create beauty out of accidents, terrible in other contexts, away from the mansion. Wealth, she realizes, transforms everything.

"The effect makes the house look even older than it is," the owner says, encouraging her to follow, to stroke the waterfall mortar as they walk.

"More than a hundred years old?" she whispers, attempting to understand the structure that is her new home, a place she will never leave. "But don't you find it's hard to imagine what happens to all that time, since houses don't age like people?"

That's when the owner tells her something she didn't want to know, something she will never forget.

"If you want to see time, to really see it in a way you'll understand, go back to my gallery of girls. To see the first girls, the girls of 1911–1920. I have a girl for every year. You're the girl of 2019."

"Where are they all?" she asks, untangling her string, re-alizing she must be careful with her body now that she's an object to be displayed in the mansion gallery for centuries, if all goes according to plan.

The architect leads her into the gallery. Near the front, most girls are her age, but as she goes farther into the long gallery, the girls get older and older and older until she begins to realize not all of them are alive.

The girls in glass cases are exquisitely preserved, but the owner is careful not to call these cases coffins. She understands without words that this is a dollhouse, and that if she calls it a cemetery, the owner will ball his soft hands into fists and tighten thin lips.

"In Japan," says the owner, "people rent hotel rooms to hold coffins before cremation. So many people are dying so much of the time. There isn't enough fire to burn all those bodies, so the dead wait in hotels, and the living wait, too."

The girl steps out of the string, which rings her ankles. When she wobbles the owner takes her elbow to steady her. "Japan," she whispers, understanding that he needs her to sound impressed, which she would be if she weren't tangled in string. "Have you been there?"

His smile flickers. "I've been everywhere. It's very dangerous outside the mansion. Girls go unprotected, wolves and knives and rubble. Even the snow is sharp in the outliers. Everything you need, everything you could ever want is right here, waiting."

The girl knows waiting, just as she knows the owner is also the architect, and his father before him, and his father's father. The long line of architect-owners with their gallery of girls,

mansions lined with ornate frames, pastel women holding little
dogs, girls in short skirts and soft shoes, pale hair and blue eyes,
seasides and high tides, prairies and poppies, forests filled with
stags and foxes, doors walled off with velvet ropes.

At the end of the longest hall in the mansion, the girl sees
a glint.

The owner-architect crooks his finger. "Come here," he
says. "You have a beautiful smile."

She follows him. They walk forever. Photos of girls turn to
sketches to glass boxes filled with torn fabric and locks of hair.

"Oh my," she murmurs, for something to say. She read a
novel once where the heroine said "Oh my" on every page.
Her mind is also tangled in string, and tightening.

He walks ahead of her, so fast she runs to catch up. Running feels uncomfortable because her loose skirt has turned
tight, leather or something like it, cinched at the waist and the
knee. She can barely breathe. Walking turns to hobbling and
then she's crawling down the longest hall in the world. She's
sorry she said yes to the ride when he pulled up beside her
outside Discount Grocery Express, where her car had broken
down in the parking lot and both paper bags split, cans of soup
rolling down the asphalt slope.

"Do you want a ride?" he asked, and she said yes. It
seemed simple; besides, saying no was a thing she wasn't good
at, was a word she never used, so yes, of course, and now
gritty cherry-scented soap in the bathroom from the cracked
dispenser, dirty tile on the floor where she crawls to the toilet
and throws up in the bowl.

"Are you alright in there?" asks the owner-architect,
knocking.

She knows what glints at the end of the hall. "You'll be the last one," he said. "So you're saving all the others. Don't you want to help other girls?"

She wants to help other girls, really she does. She was always a helper, wanted to be a nurse or a pre-school teacher.

The girl gets up and wipes vomit off her chin. Washes her hands in the rusty sink. She figures this rest stop is halfway across the country from Discount Grocery Express. They've been in his car for at least three days, hours ticking by on the dashboard clock.

"Hurry up, Doll." The doorknob rattles.

Above the sink is a mirror which covers a wall. She sees her fist as she punches glass, blood on her knuckles, as she faces the wall behind the mirror and knows she'll do anything to get through to the other side.

GIRL IN DOUBT

I MIGHT BE IN TROUBLE. I might be about to die.

I might be in trouble, serious trouble.

I can't tell if I've been abducted or not.

He's at the ATM, so there's a security camera. I'm in the car watching his hands on the money. Maybe I should run now, while his back is turned and a camera's watching his hands. Maybe he'll chase me, but I'll run faster, alley and overpass, until some safer man takes me away from this man.

Or maybe he'll come back to the car and smile, a real smile, not a creepy dead-eye glaze. With soft eyes he'll put one white hand on my knee and one white hand on the wheel, drive downtown, and take me out to dinner at that fancy vegan place I've been wanting to try. We'll both order deconstructed hijiki salad and artisanal tempeh mousse because he'll order for both of us. Laughing, picking seaweed from my teeth, he'll kiss me when he drops me off at my apartment at midnight. He won't follow me upstairs, or downstairs, because I live in the basement. He'll be long gone, off on another harmless adventure, and I'll sit with the memory of soft eyes and shy smiles.

Maybe this isn't abduction. Maybe it's a bad date that's

about to get better. Maybe there's a bouquet of eco-friendly roses waiting for me under his jacket. He'll hug me when we get to the restaurant, and I'll feel a sharp prick, but it'll be thorns to go with the roses, totally natural, romantic, and red. Not a knife, not a gun, not a dick, just thorns while he hugs me at the restaurant and says, "Table for two, please." So polite.

If he comes into my apartment, maybe he'll speak softly, so as not to wake the neighbors. Maybe he'll sit in the chair, my chair, where I read and eat chips, and I'll sit on the edge of the bed, because those are the only furniture options. Maybe sex will only happen if I say so. And maybe I'll say so or maybe I won't.

Or maybe I'm being abducted. And it won't stop with roses. He'll push me against the ugly kitchen counter, and I'll hit my head and pass out, and he'll rape me while I'm unconscious, cut my cheeks with a knife for sport, slice my skin for a trophy, and I'll wake up ripped and bleeding and go to the hospital for a rape kit, and no one will ever use it to solve this crime.

I can't tell which way this is going, A or B. I can't choose my own adventure because I'm not writing this story. I'm just waiting in the getaway car. Am I being abducted. Is this a bad date that might end with a kiss. Is he going to rape me, murder me, lock me in a shed with no food or water and torture me. Is he going to take me out to dinner. He's coming back to the car and I forgot to escape.

He opens the door, slides inside. Leather seats from an animal who gave itself up for this very moment, the moment he turns his head to look at me in the passenger seat, curled against the window because the doors were locked from out-side, and I feel his eyes on me but can't tell if they're soft or hard. I smile so wide my lips crack and bleed.

GIRL IN KNOTS [1]

WHATEVER YOU WANT. [2]

Whatever you want is what I want. [3]

Whatever you want is what I want and I want whatever you want. [4]

Whatever you want is what I want and I want whatever you want because you want it. [5]

I only want what you want. [6]

I don't want. [7]

I only want what you want, which is to give you what you want. [8]

---

[1] If you can tie a rope around your pet pig's neck, you can tie a girl who loves you. In both cases, you bind the one that trusts.

[2] My pet pig was named Domitis, walking around dominant all the time, even when it wasn't realistic.

[3] No marriage therapist wants to talk about my pet pig. Everyone wants to focus on the spanking, because that's what everyone is going home and masturbating to anyways.

[4] Right.

[5] Did I mention my pet pig could fly? I was a child then and didn't know how special Domitis was until Domitis flew away.

[6] Because you're such a nice, kind person.

[7] I don't want to talk about my flying pig anymore, unless that's what you want, since you're such a fine, upstanding citizen.

[8] That's why I'm wanted by the police now.

So I do want, but only what you want, or only what you want me to want.[9]

My wants come from you.[10]

Sometimes they're the same as your wants and sometimes different, but they're always your wants.[11]

Sometimes they're your wants for you and sometimes they're your wants for me.[12]

Sometimes those are the same things and sometimes those are different things.[13]

When I'm confused, which sometimes happens, I don't try to guess what you want because guessing upsets you. [14]

The thing you want most is for me to know what you want, whether your wants for you or your wants for me, whether those are the same or different. [15]

When I don't know, or do the wrong thing, or guess wrong, or show you I'm guessing, you get upset.[16]

When you get upset, you get angry.[17]

---

[9] Remember that time you changed my name so I didn't even know who I was anymore?

[10] As if you are another me, or as if I am becoming another you, bound to you.

[11] There's a reason why the word for "wife" in Spanish means "handcuffs."

[12] In the United States, some still call marriage "the old ball and chain."

[13] The word "esposa" comes from "spendo," meaning commitment (commercial contract), engagement, union.

[14] Wives used to stand with hands crossed in front during the marriage ceremony, exactly in the same posture prisoners are handcuffed. In the Middle Ages, people noticed the similitude between the posture and the lack of freedom commitment meant.

[15] In the early stages of marriage, handcuffs can be romantic, like jewelry, until you jump off a bridge into a river.

[16] Having survived the river, cuffed together, we swim into the ocean to watch each other, knowing if one drowns, both will perish. If one survives, both will live.

[17] At me, for loving you.

20

When you get angry, anger is what you want.[18]

When you get angry, I'm what you want, and what you want is for me to want your anger at me.[19]

When your anger goes into me, I'm what you want, and so I want your anger.[20]

When you're angry, you're violent.[21]

When you're violent, you take the rope.[22]

When I see the rope, I know you're angry. When you're angry, and I see the rope, I know you want me.[23]

The rope goes twice around my wrists and sometimes once around my ankles.[24]

Sometimes my legs are open. Sometimes my legs are tightly shut, sometimes by you, held taut by me, and sometimes by rope, and sometimes by stretching.[25]

Sometimes I'm on my back and sometimes my side, but mostly my stomach.[26]

When you're not angry, you pull me into your chest and kiss my hair and whisper my name.[27]

---

[18] Anger is less like a friend than a child you've forced me to bear.

[19] You feed anger, nurture it, holding it close so it will grow.

[20] In marriage, spousal zoochosis is preventable yet contagious.

[21] A symptom of zoochosis is violence.

[22] Neglected animals in captivity, like those in an abandoned zoo, attack their own mates, cannibalistic in zoochosis, devouring their mates and offspring when left in the cage without food.

[23] Marriage can become a cage where neglected lovers begin eating each other alive.

[24] During sex, we are sin eaters, devouring each other's regrets with flesh in intimate acts when our hunger becomes tenderness.

[25] Sometimes what hurts feels good. This is one of the greatest mysteries of pleasure.

[26] Sometimes what feels good begins to hurt. This is another of nature's mysteries.

[27] How can tenderness be so violent?

You say my name like it's something precious, song or jewel, day or night.[28]

Sometimes what I want is to start with you pulling me into your chest and kissing my hair and to stay there.[29]

You tell me I want things no one else will ever want, and how lucky I am you want what I want, which happens to be what you want, too.[30]

In the old days, when I left the house, when my feet still knew how to walk uphill, I wanted coffee at the shop on the corner, carrots and dahlias from the farmer's truck.[31]

I wanted to feel the rush of warm air in winter when I opened the door to the post office and said hello to the clerk.[32]

I wanted to mail postcards to my mother on Mother's Day.[33]

In the story someone else might tell, the postcards spell "HELP."[34]

---

[28] How can violence become tenderness?

[29] What is the difference between assault and intimacy?

[30] Where is the line between knowing someone and knowing someone too well?

[31] The one thing you never knew about me is the one thing I almost had forgotten, those dahlias wilting in the farmer's truck, a rainbow of colors in my girlhood before you turned me into another girl, different from the girl I was when you tied me in knots, making me into someone I was not.

[32] The air was freedom because I had not given myself away.

[33] Not even Mother recognizes me now. How could she? I don't recognize myself after what you've done.

[34] But the postcards are written in your hand because we both need "help" if I'm a part of you.

GIRL[35] IN PINK FLOWER[36]

IF YOU LOVE A BOMBSHELL,[37] you become a bombshell in the pink room where your breasts are pumped up, inflated with a special patent-pending boob machine[38] turning itty-bitty titties into huge pale balloons bouncing, bouncing.

No longer niblets, they aren't just globes or cantaloupes.

Now gazongas, honkers, and milk cans, your butter bags, your busters, and your bumpers are no longer love bubbles but pumpkins and pontoons.[39]

When your watermelon zeppelins rise like hot air balloons, messing with your center of gravity, you must hold onto black silk cord tied to the walls.[40]

If you float too high, you might want to wear a white velvet harness,[41] binding your knockers, leashing those puppies, strapping them down, before your girls take control of you, girl.[42]

---

[35] 18 and older

[36] Are you interested in working in the film industry? Do you dream of becoming an actress? We've got the job for you!

[37] Prior military experience preferred.

[38] Make good money working from home!

[39] Benefits include vision and dental.

[40] Flexible hours and casual Fridays are just two of the things that make working for TIT as much fun as jerking off in the sink.

[41] Supplied by your employer; however, you are responsible for dry cleaning.

[42] You go!

Your inflated skin sacks smell like fresh strawberry short-cake.[43] Your kazongas are soft and pretty with swollen nipples as pink as the walls carpeted in peony petals the color of elegantly shaved yoni in softcore dreams.[44]

Every time you are drafted into these softcore dreams, to make them into a hardcore reality, you try to reassure yourself by thinking of the isolation of tomorrow.[45]

Your people are gone now,[46] so you try to imagine all they have are portraits, still frames and video fragments to be edited in artistic views of sweat like glitter and open mouths like broken fruits where strangers are explorers going deeper and deeper inside you with their tongues and fingers.[47]

Before you realize it, there are dicks[48] everywhere, too many dicks to count, and it's too much to handle them all, to take them all in deeply enough to where they want to go inside

---

[43] Or overripe bananas and moldy yogurt left in the break room fridge.

[44] Not your dreams, obviously. In your dreams, you wear a flowing dress and walk through a field shooting your enemies with poison arrows whittled from birch.

[45] Also not your dreams, which are generally populated with people, although you are usually shooting them with poison arrows whittled from birch (see above).

[46] Not "your people," but "you people." As in, "you people can't hold down a job," or "you people are always late," or "you people are only good for one thing," or "you people the earth and everyone's still telling you to suck it."

[47] The sign on the door says "Foot Massage." The sign is neon. The sign says nothing about penetration, or tits, or a white velvet harness, or your body swollen into a giant balloon, bouncing. The sign says "Foot Massage," and there's a reflexology chart on the front door. But no one uses the front door. Everyone knows, intuitively, to use the back door, through the alley. The front door is guarded by two cruel-looking men, boys really, smoking cigarettes. These are #7 and #9 in your poison dart queue.

[48] You knew it. But you wanted so much for this story, your story, to be about tits. Flowers and pussies and velvet and tongues. But here we are, at the part where dicks enter, where the narrative gets penetrated by dick #1.

you where you let men hurt you to make everyone happy,[49] including yourself, long after you have forgotten that your clit demands its own form of justice and that justice has not been served.

No matter how much you sweat or bleed, the room doesn't smell of bleach or rust, or even semen, because of the petal walls, which are watered by nonintrusive[50] gardeners.

The room smells of lilacs and peonies opening.

Fragrant air is piped into the vents after each session[51] inside the pink flower where you start to destroy yourself and the petals, denuding the walls.

Torn petals fall like snow, clinging to violet[52] bruises.

Beneath the petals, you discover marvelous handiwork, cavepainting like hieroglyphs[53] traced in blood.

As the other girls come to haunt you with their innocent[54] smiles, their bodies bathed in light, their hair smelling of grapefruit,[55] they arrive at the house with no name, only to be trapped inside the pink flower with me, blooming.

"Excuse me, excuse me, baby," you say.

---

[49] Paper or plastic?

[50] Robots, programmed to use only as much water as needed. This genius robot will someday revolutionize almond farming in California.

[51] 30 minutes per session. 60 minutes is a double session, but they cost the same to you: too much.

[52] You're getting the idea now: you are a flower. Your skin changes color and blossoms, blooms blue and purple, and your armpits smell like dying roses, and your mouth tastes like honeysuckle whose roots are rotting from too much rain.

[53] Post to Facebook immediately. 200 likes! 2000! 20,000! 200,000 likes for the cave paintings made of blood!

[54] It's all an act.

[55] Does your hair look limp and lifeless, even after you wash? Try Petal Pearls, now in an eco-friendly, edible bag knit from hair culled from women who live in places we don't want to think about.

Strangers approach, getting nearer and nearer so our faces are touching.

No one ever backs away at tulip time[56] when they devour each other with kisses.

The girls' lips are like petals opening as the flower shrivels, withers, contracts, and fades away.

While the pink flower is dying, your breasts slowly deflate.[57]

You're moving from one gated hallway to another, when your clit awakens and stands at attention.[58]

You arrive in an aviary filled with exotic birds whose green feathers glow emerald at sundown.[59]

---

[56] IT'S ALWAYS TIME FOR TULIPS

[57] And your Tinder account stalls mid-slide.

[58] A theme song accompanies your erection. No one can hear it, not even you, but you feel the chords inside you, swelling.

[59] (cue the applause)

GIRL IN PAGEANTS[60]

AFTER ENDLESS FAD DIETS, women in magazines transform through fashionable medical procedures,[61] yet the pleasure of viewing becomes pornographic obligation at the Girl Zoo, this human dollhouse full of trophies, some taxidermized, some alive, some partially plasticized through cosmetic surgery.[62]

Toy girls are more expensive than any dolls you could ever imagine, and the price of admission into the Girl Zoo is more than a mansion costs in the hills[63] of California, well worth the price to those who want to witness the miracle of captivity.[64]

When we[65] take the new girls out of the cages, for the parade and procession on the glass stage, an anorexic beauty queen must dance with a skeletal corpse, a former professional model stuffed with hair[66] and fitted with remote-controled[67]

---

[60] Sponsored by Diet Waterberry

[61] Sponsored by Tiny Waist Paste

[62] Performed by a doctor with a diploma from a nonexistent medical college.

[63] Burning. The hills are burning, wildfires spreading, everyone drinking bottled water and roasting marshmallows.

[64] Not to be confused with the miracle of birth.

[65] "We" meaning "Exactly who you think."

[66] Pubic

[67] Also operates garage doors and that camera that lets you spy on your kids.

mechanical artificial limbs so that the corpse can spin like a ballerina in a jewelry box while the girl spins in tandem.

This exhibit is well received by men from foreign countries like America,[68] where many prominent US senators are patrons of the zoo and on its board of directors. These men say the girl's name will be Rella, and she will be transformed in an elaborate professional makeover, breast augmentation[69] with implants of cartoonish proportions so she can become a "bombshell" at the cavalcades.

In this Miss American Romance staged for the Girl Zoo, the anorexic Rella speaks in baby talk on blind dates,[70] giggling, blubbering, using pet names on a series of increasingly hideous[71] male companions, as if the double standard is a gift from God, who is also a hideous[72] man in the form of a pageant judge.

If ugliness is punishment for women in fairy tales, the judge of the Girl-Zoo beauty pageant will become the president of an English-speaking country[73] and will please himself along with other politicians by watching women onstage while asking them to masturbate[74] for an audience in a series of contests that will replace the talent[75] competition.

---

[68] Land of the freeze and home of the behave.

[69] Covered by insurance. However, future mammograms, biopsies, surgeries, radiation, chemo, mastectomies, and reconstruction will be considered pre-existing conditions and will not be covered.

[70] Sponsored by Mix-N-Mate.com

[71] We don't mean you, of course. You're very handsome.

[72] See footnote above.

[73] This is not a political allegory.

[74] Ohhh baby, give it to me! You sexy beast, you dictator, you giant orange man!

[75] Sponsored by Thin Kitten Scrapbook Pens

In these interactive televised masturbatory tournaments, prizes[76] will be given for the best self-gratification replete with multiple fake[77] female orgasms incorporating the judge's name, the top prize being a college scholarship at a for-profit university, a decade's supply of carcinogenic makeup,[78] a metallic pink convertible Hummer, six cats, and three litter boxes.[79]

Once the committee has approved the award, the president shall be appeased[80] as follows: by wedging himself into the pit of a starving woman's stomach as his eyes catch and hold with hers, begging for release to match her fake orgasms at the contests.[81]

---

[76] She is the prize.

[77] "I would never!"

[78] Produced by a conglomerate co-owned by the president's daughter.

[79] I thought you said six cats? They share?

[80] Sponsored by Cozy Ego Egg Coddlers

[81] Reelection's a sure thing, baby.

GIRL IN CAT[82]

YOU DON'T KNOW WHAT IT'S LIKE TO CHEW METAL.[83] Climbing air, in overdrive, I dove into the aviary.[84] Everything was flight and twirl.[85] You think I'm cute, but I'd twist your neck to find your pulse, toss you up until you came down mouse, and eat your eyes.[86] You don't know nature.[87] Only how to build

---

[82] When US and British media began calling Jocelyn Wildenstein the "cat woman," four million dollars of plastic surgery was just as devastating as any violent incident or freak accident like animals mutilating a woman's face. She resembled women whose lovers had thrown acid into their faces for revenge, though she paid highly trained professionals to mutilate her instead of coming by her mutilation by more common means. Like most women in zoochosis, she considered her own self-mutilation beautiful and necessary.

[83] You also don't know what it's like to feel trapped in your own body, as if you are a cat inside a girl, not a girl inside a cat.

[84] Joycelyn Wildenstein so adored big cats that she began stalking them long before she wanted surgeons to make her look like one. She was willing to pay any price for being a stalker who did not relate rationally to her prey.

[85] Joycelyn and the billionaire, who became her husband, fell in love while hunting the animals she loved. For reasons unknown, in the early stages of zoochosis, she began destroying the very beasts she most wanted to become, hunting and killing big game cats imprisoned in the billionaire's ranch. Killing cats was romantic to her and her enabler, how they bonded to each other.

[86] Around the time her billionaire husband began cheating on her with other women, she went to the world's top plastic surgeons, spending her husband's money, demanding the surgeons make her look like the big cats she and her husband once hunted.

[87] How could a woman fall in love with a man while killing the animals she loved?

a cage and suss out capture.[88] Scent of your breakfast keeps me up at night.[89] Scent of your wife.[90] I know where you live, where water goes when it storms the tap.[91] Sense the seizures in your brain, deep stealth.[92] For a moment, I was free, and ate six birds, and counted nine.[93] I left you a hole in the aviary.[94] They'll form a flock, not one behind. [95] [96]

What would make her want to transform into one of the animals she had killed just as her husband was falling out of love with her?

[88] A cat in a girl is like a girl in a cat: both kill the creatures they love.

[89] Imprisoned in her own body, nothing upsets Joycelyn like those who live happy, normal lives.

[90] Other girls make her wild, especially in the presence of her new mate, whom she has been accused of clawing and scratching.

[91] She can still see through eyes altered to wing tips?

[92] Even a multi-million-dollar condo becomes a cage, even the body becomes a prison.

[93] Avoid the food in Trump Tower, where Joycelyn lives with other trophy wives in zoochosis.

[94] Trump Tower is one of the most expensive cages for women in the world.

[95] Everyone is leaving now she is attempting to make her face look human again. To save herself, she is attempting to find the girl in the cat, not the cat in the girl. It is so hard to find her, to bring her back after her escape.

[96] Unaware of the women who love her more than their own sisters or mothers or lovers, Joycelyn will never know who they are. What beauty they see as the girl in the cat slowly emerges behind her eyes.

GIRL IN PICTURES[97]

I'm staring at Facebook,[98] trying to figure out who that girl is.[99] The girl in pictures.[100] Pictures of you.[101]

"Who's that girl?" I ask.[102]

You're brushing your teeth. You do yoga while you floss, because you hate to waste time. "What girl?"[103]

I point.

"I don't see anyone."[104]

---

[97] A girl like a hidden object is camouflaged in photographs (one of our girls, escaped from the Girl Zoo), but these two free women are too distracted to see her in their pictures. Typical of free women, they don't notice Girl-Zoo slaves, escapees in their midst.

[98] Facebook is a serious problem. To protect our agenda, surveillance and damage control are needed.

[99] We know. The problem is the other girl, behind her, in the photograph, tiny in the background.

[100] Investigation needed; after initial study, a hacker hired to erase her and an influencer already working on other subject in photo, attempting to instill aggressive behavior in those photographed, to alter communication between educated women who have the wherewithal to expose our agenda.

[101] Infiltration, undercover, inside job required.

[102] Don't say her name.

[103] How do they not see her?

[104] For some reason, no one seems to notice girls at risk. Invisible on Facebook, not as invisible on Instagram, those who escape from the Girl Zoo often disappear in plain sight.

"Right there. Smiling at the camera like she just got fucked."[105]

"I have no idea what you're talking about."[106]

Later, photos of you at some party, smiling and laughing, the girl's hand on your thigh. Then photos of you and the girl in a kayak, a tiny dog tucked under her arm.[107]

"So it's just a picture of you and a dog?"[108]

"I don't have a dog. But I went kayaking, yes, and almost drowned. Are you happy now?"[109]

You're making toast and drinking whiskey.[110] I turn on the burner for tea.

"What's her name? Hot or cold?" I go through the alphabet, starting with A.[111]

Somewhere past L you take my hand, hold it over the burner.[112] We hover, hotter.[113]

---

[105] Smiling to reintegrate. Smiling makes victims appear complicit.

[106] Possible Instagram nightmare. Facebook flub. Pinterest fiasco.

[107] Too many photos of women loving women on apps. Smartphones are the enemy. Evidence stockpile. Facebook purge activated. Lesbianism and feminism are our greatest threat, could shut down entire project. Females loving females endangers Girl-Zoo agenda.

[108] Look deeper into the background; what was accidentally captured could indict us all. Lawyers, politicians, investors, doctors, look at her eyes. Was she doing it on purpose, appearing in frame?

[109] Find a way to shut this down. The more they talk, the more they might discover about the Girl Zoo.

[110] Lesbians should be encouraged to drink whiskey, and often. It helps them forget. Send a nice bottle, aged in wooden casks of charred white oak at least ten years. Look for a medium amber with a boozy, oaky aroma, made from pure Kentucky limestone-filtered water. Nothing else will do.

[111] Someone needs to stop this game—Girl-Zoo experiment at risk.

[112] The more pain connected to the discovery of names, the better.

[113] Good result from influencer. Subject from photo behaving aggressively, as planned.

GIRL IN TENT

THE GIRL IN THE PICTURES didn't look like me at all. But you looked like you; your eyes did that thing. You were you, and she wasn't me, but each picture was posed exactly the way we'd posed for shots on our wedding day.

Actually, it wasn't a wedding. We eloped. Or escaped. We crossed the border to a country where marriage was legal, where a red-haired woman whispered our names.

The girl in the pictures was prettier than me, and younger, but obviously stupid.

You assured me you were not in love.

The girl in the pictures wrote me emails, plaintive, with a worried tone. Was I "okay." Was I "nervous," because I didn't have to be. Her parents, she said, were fine with things.

"What things are her parents fine with?" I asked.

You looked pained, or maybe tired. You'd been gone all weekend, camping entirely by yourself, hiking entirely by yourself, with only our dog for company. Which was safe, of course, to camp and hike in the woods by yourself, a girl alone.

"Are you sure you were alone? Were you alone at night? One to a tent?"

"Sweetheart, your jealousy is out of control."

But I'd seen the pictures. The light in the tent. You by the river and someone beside you. I'd seen pictures of you and the girl, marshmallows and fire, smirk floating, Cheshire.

"Sweetheart, I didn't want you to worry, but there was a bear in the tent, and it almost got me."

We were eating dinner. I passed you the bread and watched while you buttered both sides of thick slices. All I could think was how grateful I was that the bear in the tent had spared you again.

GIRL IN FREAK ACCIDENT

THE BOY ON THE BICYCLE is a man maker, not a little creep. He points the camera at the last monkey and suddenly the number one is walking into the martini shot. The number one, a teenage ape weighing over two hundred pounds and raised like a human, wears a three-piece suit over his adult diaper. The ape gets last looks from his trainer before going on camera with the young girl, a starlet. The starlet keeps laughing at the ape, won't listen to the handlers' instructions not to speak of the ape's diaper, not to laugh at the ape or to call attention to it when its diaper needs changing. Just before the freak accident, the boy follows the girl and the ape into a compound of connected houses, massive foreclosures after the bust. He doesn't know her name and doesn't want to know, until it's too late. His desire to forget what has happened and his part in it makes him lead a double life, where he dresses like her and pretends to be her onstage. All the while, he recalls her de-gloved hands reaching out to him as if he might save her.

GIRL IN RAPE KIT

I WAS ASKING WHY THEY DID IT, and my friend says they prob-
ably see us all as passive and I remembered that time I invited
him into the house and he said I can tell you don't want to do
it so I invited him back and it started with him eating me out
on the sofa and then when we got to bed he picked me up by
the ankles and impaled me so I couldn't think straight and
didn't know what to say until I saw all the blood all over his
chest and legs and asked him to stop and thought I had hurt
him and asked him if he was okay and he said I was on my period even though I wasn't and I asked him to stop, why was he
bleeding, and he was laughing because it was my blood and he
said, "I'm making love to you," and I asked him to stop and he
wouldn't so I just kept asking him to switch positions because
he was ripping me and I was trying to find a way it would hurt
me less and I asked him to stop and he wouldn't and I was never quite the same after that night he tore me apart and I didn't
even really know who he was, even though I called him once
again afterwards and never saw him again, not after I went
upstairs to take a shower and was in the shower and he came
in without knocking when I was washing off the blood and said
god, I feel like an animal, and weeks later, then there was the
other one, blonde, in finance, who asked me out for coffee and

36

then dropped me off at my house and invited himself in and I said I don't want to do it and he started taking off my clothes and then next thing I knew he had his tongue in my ass and I didn't even know his last name, would never know it and said I don't want to have sex, we're not going to have sex, and he was like all right, all right, and then was taking my clothes off, again, on the bed and then there was the liar who had sent me pictures of him in another state and when I traveled to meet him he didn't look anything like the pictures and was decades older at his studio apartment where he had two huge dogs I thought would tear me apart so I slept with my hands over my face because I was afraid they would bite me and woke to dogs pissing on the bed.

GIRL IN TREES

THE STORY GOES: he takes the girl to his apartment, which is papered in trees. The story goes. The story goes: he takes the girl. The story goes girl. The story goes the girl stays gone, buried in paper. Trees peel away from plaster and he uses glue to stick the paper back against the wall.

Once he's caught, his face all over the news, detectives snap photos of the room and publicize details, hoping more girls will step forward, girls who've been inside that room, girls who survived, who escaped with their lives, who stayed silent until now for fear he'd find them.

"It's safe now," detectives say, snapping photos. "It's safe in the room."

I'm naked, curled against the wall, against the trees on the wall, sticky with glue. I can't move. The camera flashes again. I want to tell them everything, but I'm stuck to the trees with glue and flash sears my skin and I'll never unstick.

"Start with your name," one of the detectives says.

"Monica," the voice says, and I think it's me, but it's some other girl.

"Monica," the detective says, "tell us about the girl you saw when you came to this room, when you turned and ran."

Monica has a soft voice, familiar. I remember her eyes,

and the sound of her shoes, and his rough running after. She's
pointing to trees on the wall, to the space between branches. I
want to pull myself onto the branches and climb, warmth of
birds and sun and sky.

GIRL IN TRANSIT

SHE LIVED NOWHERE, which was where he found her. Locals said her RV broke down, but it wasn't her RV and it wasn't broken. She was sleeping, they said, but she never slept in the RV. She slept in tumbleweeds. They tumbled her clothes dry and sloughed dead skin. She was in transit and he found her there, and everything after was the story he wrote.

In another chapter, his sister waited by the phone, worried. She had three kids and lived with her second husband in Grove City. She was always worried about her brother, who was always in transit, on the cups of bad news.

"Cusp," her husband corrected her.

"Cups," she said. "I know what cusp means." Her brother drank differently from the way she drank, the way her husband drank, everyone. He drank to turn into a weapon. Sometimes she worried she'd see his face as a headline. She imagined waking up, stepping outside in her bathrobe the way her father used to do, picking up the paper from the end of the driveway. Except they didn't have a driveway, and her father was dead, and newspapers came online, no rubber band, no snap, no second to prepare for the face that might glare back: YOUR BROTHER HAS COMMITTED A HEINOUS CRIME. Mostly, though, she thought about her second husband and

40

how to keep him. He had a girl already, a dancer down by the docks. A girl who didn't care about him, but took the money he gave her. And here she was, loving him, and sometimes she thought she should talk to the girl.

The girl who slept in tumbleweeds also slept at the club, and sometimes the manager let her sleep at his house. He lived in the suburbs in a house with a driveway and a husband who stayed at home with the kids. Those nights were her best, deepest dreams. She woke filled with energy and drank orange juice, watched the husband pack lunch for the kids. She would get the RV fixed and drive away from the docks and live in the flood plains out East. She would live in Chewelah. Every spring the playground would flood, water hiking the metal blade of the slide, washing the roundabout, mirroring swans who flocked in white ribbons. She would work at the library, learn yoga from YouTube, make wall hangings out of Japanese fabric, cut her hair, change her name to Ned.

To fix the RV she needed more money from the man with dead eyes whose money was wet.

One Monday night he didn't show up at the club. Instead a pretty, soft woman with pastel shoes ordered two drinks she didn't touch. Her mouth was crooked and her eyes were tired and she sat in the front row watching the girl.

The girl asked the woman if she wanted a dance.

The woman said yes.

The girl danced a few feet away, but the woman asked the girl to come closer.

The girl bent over the woman, and the woman started talking, mumbling at first, then crying.

For a moment the girl was angry. This was her job, this crying woman, and the men around her, and it cost so much. But then she thought about driving East, thought about asking the woman to come with her.

They would live in the RV and swim in the river.

They would get paid to spray orchards with pesticide, branches silver, apples white.

GIRL IN YOUR CAR

A HITCHHIKER IS ALWAYS LUCKY. You slow down because the girl by the side of the road looks lost and lonely. Looks, in other words, like you. One of you is in a car and one of you is in the rain. Then everything changes. The rain is outside, and the hitchhiker inside, fiddling with the radio dial, summoning music from static. She's kicked off her sneakers and hiked up her skirt, dirty soles resting on the dash. Smell of pot and rain and chocolate, braids tied tight with rubber bands.

You ask her name and she looks away, out the window, at the sun beginning to show across the fields, which go on forever.

You say your name is Chris.

She says her name is Chris, too. Funny. She asks how far you're willing to go.

You've never driven this road before. Something happened in town, the town you've always lived in, and you took this car, which isn't yours. There's an old ghost story kids used to tell, about a girl in white by the side of the road. On her way to a dance, or wedding, or both. How she got in a car, or carriage, and vanished.

Chris might be in white; it's hard to tell, her skirt's so dirty and the mud's so high. You talk with your hands, tracks in the field. The leaves were green and now they're pale.

A grocery store floats up to your windshield and stops. It's shaped like a farm: fake silo, fake cow. Chris smiles, gap in her teeth, something shifts in her story.

You buy two coffees, one with cream. When you get back to your car the driver's seat is littered with pink rubber bands, the kind that used to hold the news together. The silo does not produce the coffee of your dreams.

Sipping coffee, you go over your collection. For years, you've saved articles of "kids" who came home after long periods of time: five months, nine months, six years, 8 years, 12 years, 23½ years. You might become one of those "kids" someday and so might the other runaways, the missing hitch-hikers. If only you could remember who I am, who you are, and who the girl in your car once was.

In your dreams, you drive her back home, to take her back where she belongs. Along the way, you remember who you are, even though you'll never remember who I am. That would be a mistake. Your mind must protect you from me.

Who did I used to be? Where did I come from? What makes me do the things I do?

I'm a repressed memory. Your mind can't handle knowing me.

The girl in your car is the answer to a question you forgot to ask.

The question disappears with the answer when she leaves you on the road to nowhere.

GIRL IN ORGAN

BECAUSE SLEEPING INSIDE this old church organ is better than sleeping inside a coffin, I burn a little candle in antique dust.

It's not easy to be homeless, especially inside a church.

People don't appreciate those who invade the house of God.

They would rather have me dead than living inside a house I can't afford.

If you can't afford to love me, please let me live inside your hymns and psalms.

I'm the girl inside the organ where each barrel is activated to play the instrument mechanically, each barrel with hymns touched by whispers of breath.

I take deep breaths, breathing in time, with a pedal on either side of my hands.

One day, if you are kicked out of all the places you know and have no one to take you in, a shadow box might become your home. You might build a nest like the one I've built inside the church's organ, a nest of dust, disintegrating hymnals, and songs our people sang long ago.

GIRL[114] IN ATROPHY[115]

IF[116] THE PLACEBO IS A SHAM PILL, the birds will eat it.[117] But I will find no relief.[118]

After slipping inside me,[119] the doctor's gloved fingers cross from bone to thigh.[120] My injured limbs have atrophied from long disuse, and no one will tell me why.

Nurses[121] wash my legs and lower body because I cannot move down there.[122] It's part of the wasting process, my paralysis, the muscles[123] going through lack of use.

Grime floats in my[124] washbowl at the hospital where I take my daily sponge baths. Scabs, pus, and sweat bob on soapy water, graying.[125]

---

[114] Patient 3R Trial 74D6P

[115] Or "Girl Trophy"

[116] The word "if" suggests that the patient understands simple logic.

[117] This is false.

[118] Patient appears prone to malignant narcissism.

[119] Normal examination procedure

[120] Patient's obvious desire for the doctor contributes to her body's dissolution and suggests that her ability to think for herself is deteriorating.

[121] Here, as elsewhere, "nurse" means "female."

[122] Here, as elsewhere, patient exaggerates her condition.

[123] If the reader is dyslexic, the word "rainbow" appears in this line.

[124] Note the patient's possessiveness: "my washbowl," "my baths." What a bitch.

[125] Gray hair contributes to women's diminished sense of taste.

Men in scrubs fight for position at the door,[126] and now I'm suffering sexualized exhaustion.[127]

My labia are torn for reasons unknown.[128] What I can't remember has harmed me worse than what I can.[129]

I don't even know how I got here or why.[130] I don't even know why the nurses lock the door when they leave my room.[131]

One nurse says to the doctor,[132] whose gloved hands are covered in my blood, "Be careful. She'll fall in love with you."[133]

Syphilis and gonorrhea are pink creatures,[134] uninvited friends, who were once visitors having overstayed their welcome like snakes hiding in my roses as I read *Leaves of Grass*.[135]

I'm reading *Leaves of Grass* when I feel a pain down there again and reach out to hold it, reaching and grabbing the pain without thinking.[136] My labia finally fall apart, falling away from me as I grab what's hanging off, pulling tattered meat and hide.[137]

I hold the rotten petal in my trembling hands, then go back to reading a long poem.[138]

---

[126] The emoji depicting this ritual shows three heads peering out of a doorframe.

[127] Patient repeatedly confuses sex with exhaustion.

[128] This is false. The reasons are known, but the persons are unknown.

[129] True

[130] False

[131] Patient is lying. She knows why. She knows very well why.

[132] Here, as elsewhere, "doctor" means "male."

[133] Love serves as a ritual of permission.

[134] Technically false

[135] Although her choice of reading material is suspect, the patient's ability to read suggests the possibility of normal brain activity.

[136] Moment of religious conversion

[137] She's just a piece of meat.

[138] Reading out loud, a form of pleasure that should be discouraged in the future. Make note: take her books away.

GIRL IN ZOO

I HATE SEEING ANIMALS dressed in human clothing but feel differently about seeing humans dressed as animals.

In the Girl Zoo, I am the walrus.

My friend Rachel is the zebra.

Gemma is the panther.

Zoe is the lioness. I remember her exhibit called "Girl in Lioness."

When the lioness became pregnant, keepers said the cubs would fetch a good price throughout the world because their father was the president's son, who dressed in the mane. According to those who study lions in the wild, the couple copulates twenty to forty times a day, often foregoing eating.

We make a lot of money in here, working in restricted areas.

GIRL IN BOX

OUR GIRLS WERE DISAPPEARING. Missing from backyards, bunk beds, and basketball courts. Missing on roller skates, tight-ropes, and milk cartons. The girls were disappearing, but not my girl, fuck no, hell no, not now, not ever. I said it over and over. I said it while I watched her riding the bus, reading to hamsters, imitating elephants. While she slept I watched over, first in ordinary ways, then fierce, never blinking. I couldn't look away, not for a second, because she might disappear.

First I walked her to and from the bus, kicking dust. Then I rode behind the bus to school. Then I drove her to school, then I homeschooled her.

I told her read this.

I told her stay inside.

I told her don't answer the door when I'm gone, which is never.

I made her sleep on a trundle under my queen, then in a sleeping bag, then in a box. I tied her to things when we went out, Houdini'd benches and streetlamps with bicycle locks, deadbolts, and handcuffs. I kept the key in my coat, spare in my sock, left sole, where it grooved into skin.

One night we needed bread, but when I locked her in her box she seemed unhappy. We were so close, like siblings more than what we were. She wasn't speaking by then, but I knew what she needed.

O metal cuff around the bench outside Glen's Market. She lay on the sidewalk, sprawled in chalk, so I tucked her legs under her, moved her hands to make it seem like she was playing with gravel. Inside I raced around, soup and bread and bottled water. I stashed supplies in my pockets and slipped out the door.

O other cuff clattered, clunked on the sidewalk where they must've greased her girlwrist and grabbed her, easy as air, girl missing from the marketplace tableau I'd arranged so carefully. Cans of minestrone soup and a sesame baguette tumbled from my coat.

I walked back to my apartment and cleaned her box, in case she decided to come home, even to visit. I was only borrowing when I took her. I knew she'd go, claw her way back to where she came from. I knew someday I'd find another, borrow her longer, make missing mine.

GIRL IN REFRIGERATOR [139]

Because it's cold inside, so cold,[140] I sleep a lot in here, partly because it's always dark when the door closes.[141]

I don't know why he put me in here.[142] He said I was bad.[143] So were some of the others. My temper, he said, ran too hot. Now I must be in the cold, near the meat because I might spoil.[144]

Wedged between shelves, my pillow[145] is a package of ground round. I cuddle up to cabbage and cheese. On the shelf above, a carton[146] of milk.[147]

The light hurts my eyes[148] as he opens the refrigerator door to reach for the milk, and he looks at me as if I am meat[149] now,

---

[139] See also: oven, freezer, washer, dryer.

[140] Repetition is a symptom of zoochosis. Other symptoms include: gnawing on metal, scratching skin with fingernails, picking at scabs, tearing out hair strand by strand.

[141] Sweet dreams.

[142] They know. It's instilled from the start: you will be caught.

[143] Not the opposite of good.

[144] Spoil, meaning both "rancid" and "brat."

[145] Why is she complaining? She has a pillow and a bed.

[146] See the photograph, the missing girl? That girl is long gone. Now drink.

[147] Note her attraction to milk, which she is made of, and for.

[148] In the age-progression photos, her eyes are lined.

[149] Meat, as in what's bred for flesh.

twisting me,[150] shoving me aside to make room[151] for another girl.[152]

---

[150] Pragmatic. Not for sport.

[151] Rooms. Refrigerator as dollhouse. Open the door and all becomes visible.

[152] We call this "company."

GIRLS IN BARS

I. GIRL IN DAIQUIRI

She's Flor de Caña, simple syrup, and freshly squeezed limes. I'm American moonshine and RumChata. One of our girlfriends is Skittles infused with vodka. The other is Gold schläger and Rumple Minze: fire and ice. Her mother is Bunny Guinness: coffee liqueur with Carolans Irish Cream and Goldschläger. My sister is a Gladiator Bomb: amaretto and SoCo dropped into Sprite and OJ. Meanwhile, her sister is a Thunder Bomb: Stoli Vanil vodka and Blue Curaçao dropped into orange Fanta. She kisses me like strawberries and cream: Bacardi, Malibu, amaretto, strawberries, and coconut milk. She spins me into a tropical smash: amaretto, Captain Morgan, Malibu fresh pineapple, fresh-squeezed OJ, house sweet and sour, and cherry juice. She breathes her breath into me, then licks my lips like a piña colada—Malibu rum, dark rum, amaretto, simple syrup, fresh pineapple, and coconut milk. "Hey, America," she whispers. Now, I'm house-made cinnamon apple moonshine.

II. GIRL IN GARAGE-STYLE MIMOSA

Smell the wild thyme from the lakeshore as girls in bars whisper to each other, aware we are listening. We were once their mothers but are strangers now. Their laughter becomes like blossoms flown on the wind, later blown through air vents as the girls become like pollinators in the greenhouse where they kiss each other, becoming women they think are so different from the ones who were once their mothers. Do they ever remember us as they drink garage-style mimosas: vodka, champagne, and freshly squeezed orange juice? They drink and drink, never realizing we are confined with sweet-smelling flowers, hot-house women sweating near the gardener, who mists our bodies in clingy gowns, while observers wearing scissor spectacles regard us as if we are merely flowers blooming in cottage-garden paintings.

III. Girl in Summer Toddy

Jack Daniel's, honey, rosewater, and freshly squeezed lemon: party planners asked us to fill bathtubs with this concoction and called it the "whiskey dance."

My lover and I bathed in it, night after summer night.

Soon, we began filling the kiddie pool with the new old fashioned—rye whiskey, house bitters, orange bitters, and simple syrup.

Once my lover's hair was slicked back in simple syrup, rosewater misted my eyes, and we kissed.

A halo of bees followed us down the stairs where honey stuck to the rails.

Bees floated past our eyes, hovering, as she whispered.

Orange bitters dripped from our breasts, although my lover assured me my breasts were coated in lemon.

We did the whiskey dance on those summer nights of our captivity. Between my legs, I felt her heart fluttering. I came, shuddering, drunk on what I thought was love, always wondering. What if I was wrong to believe her heart was throbbing as we retreated?

She kissed me, cradling my face in her hands. I never wanted summer to end. As she released me, I felt her fingers slowly drifting away from my eyes with bees combing the apple orchards.

GIRL IN HOT CAR

SOMETIMES WHEN WE'RE IN THE CAR she needs to stop, get gas, get groceries, go to the bathroom, make a call. Sometimes she unrolls the windows and pats me on the head and says, "Back soon." I sit by the window, panting. Waiting for her to decide if I'll die.

She leaves me water, but the water gets hot, hotter than my tongue. Outside, people and dogs move past me, swimming in waves of heat. I'm burning up, ear wax melting, eyes dry and nose bleeding. I taste blood on my tongue, in the back of my throat.

When she comes back, she takes her time arranging groceries in the trunk of the car while I slide off the seat. Then she beeps the door unlocked, but stops to check her phone. Finally she opens the door, adjusts the mirror, keys the car humming. It's almost time for the cool breeze, for my tongue to unswell, for my breath to unbuckle. But first, in the boiling heat, she turns on the radio and scans all the songs.

GIRL IN ONE-ACT PLAY

ANIKA APPEARS TO BE ALONE ONSTAGE, sitting in a chair, talking to herself.

ANIKA: The girl was so good in the car. Sometimes the dog barked, but the girl never cried. Well, not never. Once Jenny and I were yelling at each other, yelling the old way, the way we thought the girl would fix. And she started crying, this high-pitched siren. Like she couldn't fix the broken thing. We'd gone to the zoo; I mean the day Jenny and I started fighting again. We hadn't had a fight in months. But it had all just gone underground. We'd been so busy with the girl, with living. We'd been too busy to fight about Chris.

Light illuminates the man sitting across from Anika.

OFFICER: Chris?

ANIKA: I'm sorry.

OFFICER: Chris?

ANIKA: The person Jenny was sleeping with. Out in the open. Everyone knew. I wanted Jenny to stop sleeping with Chris. It's like breaking your diet. Once you start, you might as well keep going. Not that I diet; I mean, I resist those cultural messages. I'm going to teach my ...

OFFICER: (offers coffee-stained napkin to Anika)

ANIKA: (brushes away napkin) The fight at the zoo wasn't important. It was just the day we started fighting again.

OFFICER: I understand. On the day of the incident, Jenny took a different route to work.

ANIKA: You keep calling it "the incident."

OFFICER: What would you like me to call it?

ANIKA: Isn't that your job? To name things?

OFFICER: It's my job to—

ANIKA: Make up stories about Lizard.

OFFICER: Lizard was your daughter's nickname?

ANIKA: What do you think? That we named her Lizard? You're looking for more evidence of what terrible mothers we were.

OFFICER: I'm gathering information about the incident.

ANIKA: "The incident" again. Why don't you call things by their names?

OFFICER: Is there a word you'd rather use?

ANIKA: It was an accident. Call it that.

OFFICER: I understand.

ANIKA: You can't possibly understand.

OFFICER: I understand. I mean, I understand that I don't understand.

ANIKA: Thank you for not understanding.

OFFICER: Did the explosion on Greenwood Avenue factor in? Difficulty sleeping, stress?

ANIKA: After the explosion we thought we were safe. Like our bad luck got used up on that one thing.

OFFICER: Would you say you were a careful parent?

ANIKA: I was bad cop; Jenny was good cop. Oh. Sorry.

OFFICER: No offense, ma'am. I consider myself a good cop. How did you approach—how did the two of you go about having a child?

ANIKA: Do you want to start with the egg? You want to start with the sperm.

OFFICER: I'm sorry if I asked—

ANIKA: We got pregnant in Florida. Jenny wanted to bring home a lizard, sneak it through security. For good luck. Like a lizard's a souvenir, a T-shirt, or a postcard. Like a lizard's not a living thing. So I said no, and we had a fight in the hotel, and she stormed off to a bar, and that's where—

OFFICER: Jenny was the real mother, then?

ANIKA: We were both real mothers.

OFFICER: Birth mother, I mean. I'm sorry. I'm not up on the lingo. Continue? Please.

ANIKA: Jenny fucked some guy, a stranger, and got pregnant with Lizard in a bar in Palm Beach.

OFFICER: Was your wife—

ANIKA: "Wife" still sounds strange. I bet you say it all the time.

OFFICER: Was your wife—

ANIKA: Do you say the word "wife" without thinking about it? Does it slide off your tongue?

OFFICER: Was your wife—

ANIKA: Your wife. What's her name?

OFFICER: That isn't … Marie.

ANIKA: We were domestic partners, and the state rolled us over. The state made our partnership into a marriage after DOMA was repealed. We woke up and we were wives. We didn't create it. It happened to us.

OFFICER: On the day of the incident—

ANIKA: Did you have a registry? You and Marie?

OFFICER: On the day of the incident—

ANIKA: Wine glasses, blender, those little forks for stabbing corn?

OFFICER: On the day of the incident—

ANIKA: I love it when people say "no gifts," and everyone brings money in a silver envelope decorated with bells. Did you and Marie—

OFFICER: Stop asking about Marie.

ANIKA: Sorry. Officer.

OFFICER: On the day of the incident, Jenny's car was in the shop. She took Lizard's—what was your daughter's proper name?

ANIKA: Taylor Astrid.

OFFICER: Taylor.

ANIKA: Astrid. Astrid was mine.

OFFICER: Taylor Astrid. It's a beautiful name.

ANIKA: No, it's not. They cancel each other out. "Taylor" and "Astrid" don't belong to the same person. She was torn in half, there at the naming. She didn't have a chance. Astrid was my Swedish grandmother's name. She lived in Trosa. "Trosa" means "women's underpants."

OFFICER: I see.

ANIKA: I come from Swedish chicken farmers. We get up. We feed the chickens. We drown our kittens in the well.

OFFICER: Would you say that your daughter added joy or stress to your life?

ANIKA: My daughter was my life.

OFFICER: Would you say that your marriage added joy or stress to your life?

ANIKA: I used to watch Jenny read at night, hair falling in her eyes. Watch her lips move. I never stopped feeling that way. At the trial I still—I still wanted to be close to her. But she sat by herself.

OFFICER: On the day of the incident, Jenny's car was in the shop. She took Taylor's car seat—

ANIKA: Call my daughter by her name.

OFFICER: Of course. Which name do you … Okay. She took Astrid's car seat and put it in the rental car.

ANIKA: Car-a-Mile. It sounds like candy.

OFFICER: Carmel.

ANIKA: No, sweeter. "Mile" sounds sweeter than "mel."

OFFICER: Mile. Mel.

BOTH: Car-a-Mile. Car-a-mel.

ANIKA: Sweeter.

OFFICER: I see your point. On the day of the incident, Jenny took the car seat and put it in the back of the Car-a-Mile. Then she drove to work, but she took Aurora instead of Greenwood because construction was still blocking traffic on Greenwood, due to the pipeline explosion a few weeks earlier.

ANIKA: That's right.

OFFICER: It says here that Jenny called in late to work. Your address was 523 Dayton, correct?

ANIKA: Yes.

OFFICER: You'd been out of town for a week on business, scheduled to come back that night—

Anika: (nods her head)

OFFICER: and someone stayed with Jenny while you were—

ANIKA: No one stayed. Just Jenny and Astrid.

OFFICER: Someone named Chris.

ANIKA: Chris came to our house? That day?

OFFICER: No, Chris arrived the evening of the day you left—

ANIKA: and stayed.

OFFICER: Sometimes after an incident—

ANIKA: Accident. Accident, Astrid, Aurora. You're missing all the A's.

OFFICER: On the morning of the accident, Jenny called in late to work because—

ANIKA: Chris saw her, then.

OFFICER: Her car wouldn't start. Then Jenny took the rental car with Astrid—

ANIKA: You think you know someone. Chris said goodbye to

my daughter after I did. Chris was the second-to-last person to see her alive.

OFFICER: New information—

ANIKA: What good does knowing do? How do I go back?

OFFICER: Maybe Chris wanted—

ANIKA: It's like those women who marry serial killers—the white dress, the house in the suburbs. Then one day the sheriff shows up with a backhoe. You think you know someone. Then you learn they're in love with their BDSM play partner. Then you learn what a BDSM play partner is. Then your daughter dies, and you pull out all your hair, and start eating dirt.

OFFICER: Once I left my gun at Starbucks. The barista ran into the street and almost got hit by a truck. Double homicide later that day, but not with my gun, and my coffee was perfect.

ANIKA: It's not funny.

OFFICER: Sometimes the joke is just telling the truth.

ANIKA: It was an accident. It could happen to anyone. A few years ago there was an increase in accidents. Because child safety laws changed. Air bag deaths when kids sat in the front. So everyone put their kids in the back, in car seats, faces turned away. Sometimes we forget what we can't see. Different parts of the brain compete. The part that remembers competes with the part that has to forget, that needs to forget in order to focus. In order to drive, to navigate all the details we take for granted—stop signs, lights, red, yellow, green. How many minutes ahead we've set the clock on the dash. The name of the client at our first meeting. If the boss likes coffee black. There's a push now for safer cars. For an alarm that goes off if your child is still in the car seat after you've turned off the engine. But it's slow, the movement. Slow because people don't want to admit it could happen to them. But everyone makes mistakes. Everyone forgets and later, remembers. What happens after that is random, good luck or bad. People forget, but the weather holds and nothing happens. Nothing at all. People forget, and their kids sleep in their car seats, don't even wake up, never know, and maybe it goes unspoken. People run red lights, slip on ice, make peanut butter sandwiches and kill other people. I can't blame Jenny for something I might've done, you might've done. An accident.

OFFICER: You filed for divorce a year after it happened.

ANIKA: I filed for divorce because Jenny loved Chris. Loves Chris. Present tense. I lost my daughter and I lost my wife. She offered to stay. To split her time between me and Chris. Thought she was being generous when she offered me weekends. Jenny always had a plan. But I couldn't live with half a marriage. I'd rather be alone. So you know what her version of our story is?

OFFICER: (shakes his head)

ANIKA: That I left her. "I can't believe you left me," she said. She said, "I would never have left you." Because she offered me half the week. Because loving someone else, fucking someone else—somehow, that didn't count as leaving. I wouldn't have left her even though she killed our daughter. At first my anger swallowed me alive. I tried to find out where Chris worked. I didn't know anything about this person, this person Jenny loved. Loves. Who she was. Is. If Chris even existed. Exists. I wanted to kill her. Kill myself. And then I realized I was angry at Jenny.

OFFICER: So now you're angry at Jenny. Not at Chris.

ANIKA: Being angry at Chris is like licking frosting off a knife. But I'm not angry at Jenny now, either. I can't stay angry. If I let myself feel my anger, I'd destroy the whole fucking world. Can I tell you something? Something I've never told anyone?

OFFICER: (sips coffee)

ANIKA: Sometimes, I mean, it's only happened once or twice, three times—sometimes I think I made the whole thing up. Not just Jenny and Chris, but Lizard, too. Like my life was never real. It always seemed too good, like I didn't deserve it. After the accident I drove to Amit's house. My high school boyfriend. I showed up on his doorstep and knocked and knocked and his mother answered and I asked about prom. I guess my brain just took a vacation. Like Palm Beach in winter. Can you imagine? I'm standing on the stoop, knocking on his door, waiting for my corsage, my first dance under fake stars. The theme was Cornucopia of Constellations. Which makes absolutely no sense.

OFFICER: Themes never do.

ANIKA: I talked to his mom and kept asking where Amit was, why I couldn't see him. "He has a job," she said, like that explained it. While I was talking she dialed 911. At first they thought I was drunk. Then they realized I was that lady. The one on the news, screaming in the parking lot. I dream about Lizard, wake up thinking she's still alive. Sometimes I try to call her on the phone, as if she could talk, as if she ever spoke, but she was too young, and now she's dead.

OFFICER: Eleven months—

ANIKA: I got off work early. Because it was Friday, and the first hot day. Everyone was headed to Gas Works Park or Alki Beach, but I didn't care about the view. I just wanted to surprise my Lizard. My little girl. I drove to the daycare and parked and knocked on the door—it was yellow, everyone's always so pleased with the sun, but I like the rain, blue-gray swells on the Sound. The door was yellow. Tasha came out holding Jason on her hip. Dante stood behind Tasha and Jason, holding Sierra's hand.

He said, "Hey, Anika, we missed Lizard today. We missed her, didn't we Sierra?"

And I said, "Lizard's here."

Dante said, "I don't think so, but let me check with Tasha."

Tasha was standing right there, holding Jason. She looked confused. "No Lizard."

"She's here."

"Lizard's not here. Is she with Jenny?"

"She's here. Jenny dropped her off."

Tasha said, "No."

Dante said, "Sorry."

And I knew.

I knew.

So I just left. Didn't say anything else. I think they knew, too. I think we all did. They came to the funeral, Tasha and Dante, and they came because they knew in the same moment I did. We all felt it. There's a knowing, a place you enter. A room. Later I wondered why I didn't stop it. Why I didn't think of something else. I mean, the knowing felt so firm. My fault, as if just knowing was what made her go. Later I wondered whether maybe, if I'd thought of something else, some other reason, like Take Your Daughter to Work Day, or Jenny home sick, or even Jenny leaving me for Chris, Jenny and Chris and Lizard all kidnapping each other in the Car-a-Mile—later I wondered whether maybe if I'd thought some other thought, it might've come true. I worried I killed her by thinking I knew. But I did. We all three felt it. So I raced out of there, so fast, I don't remember but they tell me how fast, and I drove to Tech-Sound. Looked for the Car-a-Mile. So many. Like five or twenty. I had to park in the guest lot and walk to the main parking lot. But I ran. Ran to the first one, blue—not that one—ran to the second one, gray—another blue one—fourth one—fifth one. It was the sixth. The sixth car was red. I think I knew she picked a red one. The sixth one was red. My daughter inside. By then five hours. The sun. All day. It never does, the sun never shines here. All it does in Seattle is rain. Gray skies might've saved her. I could see but I couldn't touch. So I dumped my bag on the ground and searched for the spare key to Jenny's car, forgetting it wasn't Jenny's car at all. Forgetting. And I tried the key to Jenny's car, kept trying to unlock. Wrong key. Wrong car. Kept trying to unlock the door. It was so hot that I stopped breathing. Screamed, they tell me. I don't remember a thing after that.

OFFICER: A gun.

ANIKA: What gun?

OFFICER: A gun goes off. And sometimes the kickback is all you remember.

ANIKA: I've never owned a gun. But I had a daughter.

OFFICER: Forgetfulness can be a gift.

ANIKA: A gift? I want to see. I'd give anything to see her face.

OFFICER: Sometimes we forget what our bodies can't handle. Our brains protect it. Store the memories inside.

ANIKA: A gift? What the fuck is wrong with you, gifting? I can't remember what she looked like. All I can see is the red car, and keys, and someone breaking the window. And Jenny, running out the door—

OFFICER: A gun goes off. Someone shoots a gun and the bullet hits, but the shooter feels numb.

ANIKA: We make assumptions all the time. We assume we'll see the ones we love again, but we don't know.

OFFICER: We don't. Maric

ANIKA: I keep trying to remember. If I forget, it's my fault, too.

If I can forget my daughter's face, I could've left her in the car. I'm no different. It's my accident, too.

OFFICER: I just went numb when the gun went off.

ANIKA: What are you talking about? There's no gun in this story.

OFFICER: When I'm in a room, there's always a gun.

ANIKA: This is a story about me and my wife. The daughter we had and the life we lost.

OFFICER: You speak as if it's your fault, somehow. If I were you, I'd be angry at Jenny.

ANIKA: Angry?

OFFICER: It was an accident, but you have every right to your feelings.

Door opens. Security enters.

SECURITY: How's it going in here?

OFFICER: We're fine. We're getting the job done.

SECURITY: May I speak with you for a minute?

They step outside. Anika takes out a pack of cigarettes. Looks around nervously. Lights up, smokes. Waits a moment, then grabs his notebook. The notebook is blank. She's confused.

ANIKA: Nothing at all. White on white. (hears noise, puts notebook back)

They enter the room.

SECURITY: Well, then, I'll leave you to it. Just making sure everything's in order.

OFFICER: Of course. Thank you.

Security leaves.

ANIKA: Why haven't you written anything down?

OFFICER: No smoking inside the station.

ANIKA: (stares at him)

OFFICER: (looks down)

ANIKA: (hands him the cigarette)

OFFICER: (takes a drag, then stubs it out on the table)

ANIKA: Why haven't you written anything down?

OFFICER: I don't need—

ANIKA: Who uses a notepad anymore? Where's your computer? This doesn't feel right to me. (gets up, walks to door, puts hand on doorknob)

OFFICER: Wait.

ANIKA: It's just not right.

OFFICER: Okay, I can explain.

ANIKA: I'm not a prisoner. The door's unlocked. I can leave anytime.

OFFICER: Of course you can. Just a follow-up interview. Strictly voluntary.

ANIKA: Voluntary?

OFFICER: You're free to leave at any time.

ANIKA: Voluntary? You asked me here to talk about the worst thing that's ever happened to me, every parent's worst fear, the most horrific—You asked me here to talk about it all over again after three years of nightmares and pills and—This is me doing you a favor. I don't want to talk. I don't want to remember. It's been almost three years and I want to forget. I want five minutes where I don't think about a fistful of keys.

OFFICER: I can explain. It's not what it looks like.

ANIKA: It doesn't look like anything. You called me here. You said this was part of the file on Jenny. I don't love her anymore, but I did love her, and what she did was an accident. An accident. And the judge was right to let her go. Anyone can forget. You, me, Marie—

OFFICER: No more about Marie.

ANIKA: Why did you call me?

OFFICER: It's part of my plan.

ANIKA: A man with a plan. Is this some sort of experiment to see how much pain you can put me through before I snap? Are you even a cop?

OFFICER: (holds up his badge)

ANIKA: That looks fake.

OFFICER: Because it's real.

ANIKA: You should've called Jenny. It was always about her anyway: her guilt, her grief, her loss. Because she's the birth mother and birth mothers mourn. Are you in AA? Are you making amends?

OFFICER: I'm on probationary desk duty. They took my gun. I called because I need help. Can't sleep, can't drive. Marie says—Marie says if I don't get help—

ANIKA: You think I'm the help?

OFFICER: It sounds wrong when you say it.

ANIKA: Your notebook's blank because it's not about me.

OFFICER: Sometimes I can't breathe. Marie says—

ANIKA: My wife killed our daughter. I tried to save her. Tried to break the windows of the car. When I got to the hospital, my hands were bleeding. My nails were torn. I'd scraped the keyhole with my fingers. Pounded the windows. I attacked the car like it wanted to take me. My daughter. Inside.

OFFICER: I know how it feels to want to go back—

ANIKA: You have a gun. I'm just a mother.

OFFICER: Marie—

ANIKA: Stop talking about Marie. You have no idea about marriage. How it feels to be denied, over and over. How your relationship means nothing. Not a goddamn thing. For so long. And then suddenly, boom, gunshot goes off and you're married. And everything's supposed to be easy. You're supposed to know what to do. How to be a wife, how to be a mother. And then how to divorce. How to untangle ties you didn't choose. We were together in a different way. The old way. The way queers have always—You wouldn't understand. There was a community. We loved each other and we fucked. But we didn't do this thing called marriage and look where it got us. Everyone's getting divorced, all my friends, none of us were made for this—this thing. You made this thing. And you kept it from us, and then strangled us with it.

OFFICER: I have no idea what you're talking about.

ANIKA: A gun goes off. Someone falls to the ground. You outline the body in chalk, in white. And when they move the body, the outline stays. After Lizard died, Jenny and I were just empty, hollow. An outline. We didn't know how to be married. But Jenny had Chris. At least she had that. So I let her, I just—I didn't even try to stop them.

OFFICER: But it's not like you were really—you know—

ANIKA: Really what?

OFFICER: Together. I mean, you were just—

ANIKA: Friends?

OFFICER: You said yourself you weren't really married.

ANIKA: We were really together. We loved and we fucked. And our daughter is dead.

OFFICER: I'm not a bigot.

ANIKA: I'm not saying you are. I'm saying that marriage wasn't the structure we chose. We had ways of loving that were outsider ways. And the state changed us. Made us more like you. You and Marie. Your wife. That word.

OFFICER: Everyone's an outsider somewhere. They know, the guys. I used to be one of them. But now I'm just a paper pusher. A secretary, like I'll start wearing a skirt.

ANIKA: Did you hear what you just said?

OFFICER: They look at me funny. But that's not why. That's not why you're here. It's the grief—the guilt—

ANIKA: Who did you shoot?

OFFICER: I can't—

ANIKA: Why not? You've read my file. You know where I live, my dead daughter's name.

OFFICER: Pending investigation.

ANIKA: Have you talked to anyone?

OFFICER: You wouldn't understand.

ANIKA: Try me.

OFFICER: Marie says if I don't—If I don't get help she'll—

ANIKA: Leave.

OFFICER: If she leaves I can't—

ANIKA: Marie loves you. She loves you, that's all. She's sending you a message. A message and you have to reply. Like when someone texts. You don't leave them hanging. You text back, little bubbles, and they see them, and they know you're there.

OFFICER: I stand in the kitchen—

ANIKA: She wants to know you're there—

OFFICER: I forget where I am—

ANIKA: And not a chalk outline—

OFFICER: I took the tablecloth once. It was white, white cotton. She says I pulled it off the table and put it on the floor. I was shaking. I covered the body but when she lifted the cloth there was nothing there.

ANIKA: (reaches for his hand)

OFFICER: (pulls away) I don't deserve your compassion. You're innocent. You're on that side of the line. Once you've crossed it, you can't go back. I'm not supposed to say I'm guilty. But I can't forget.

ANIKA: You're not a monster. Everyone makes mistakes. It's been three years. Why did you call me?

OFFICER: I asked you because I need to forget. And in order to forget I need your forgiveness.

ANIKA: Why me?

OFFICER: You forgave Jenny, so you'll forgive me.

ANIKA: I don't even know you. I have no idea what you did, or why, or if it was justified. I don't even know what justified means. But forgiveness is supposed to be unconditional. I mean, if I can forgive Jenny, I can forgive you. Officer—wait. What's your name?

OFFICER: (writes it down, slides the paper across the table)

ANIKA: (looks up at him, back down at the paper) Your name is Chris?

Fade to black.

GIRL IN CENTERFOLD

THIS PIECE SHOULD SPAN the middle of the book, two pages opening flat like a centerfold.

This piece should be glossy. Also, it should have a scratch 'n sniff patch, ideally covering the model's crotch.

Also, she shouldn't be a model. This should be the author photo, but since there are two authors it should be a collage, a composite of their best features: Aimee's face, obviously, and Aimee's legs. Carol's left breast, Aimee's right. Carol's ears.

Each body part should be photographed, outlined, examined, compared, cut, and then pieced back together again.

At book signings, both authors should sign the center-fold instead of the title page. Also, the scratch 'n sniff feature should be a perfume sample, followed by perfume ads on the pages before and after the centerfold.

Aimee's stomach, Carol's ass.

The pages lie flat, tits on one page, pussy on the other.

When the book shuts, the composite girl licks her wounds in the silence of stitches.

See how she asks for this, to be read so easily. No longer an author but the girl trapped inside.

TWO

GIRL IN LIBRARY

CORINNE

For a while, between husbands, I slept with one of my coworkers. I picked her because she had a beautiful mouth and no social media presence. She picked me because I was short, which she said made it easier to sleep on her mattress. She was seventy-two, my grandmother's age, which could've been weird, but I liked my grandmother, and besides, she wasn't actually related. It just felt that way because we'd read the same books. Daphne's age was the least interesting thing about her. The most interesting thing was that she'd read every book in the library. Granted, it was a small-town library, but still. She spent so much time reading that she had no other life. She slept under the reception desk, on a twin bed hidden by curtains. The staff break room had a hot plate on which she cooked delicious meals: curries, stir frys, omelets. I don't know where she showered, but she smelled and tasted incredible. I was madly in love with the librarian, and never imagined she'd break my heart.

DAPHNE

The lady who ran the library, she was young and had a marijuana tree about six feet high, until someone found it and cut it. She was pissed because she had nurtured it, adoring the tree, the beautiful way it flowered. She really babied the damned thing, pampering it with kisses on leaves, whispers on blossoms. She would climb a ladder and trim it, before someone hacked it from the ground. After it was stolen, there wasn't much the young librarian could do, except for have sex with me because, when she felt sad, I could release her. I mourned the marijuana tree the only way I knew how, by putting my tongue deep inside her where I could taste everything, including her pain. I was the old librarian, and we did this repeatedly, hiding in stacks of books that smelled deliciously of delicate mold.

CORINNE

My job was standing in front of the reception desk. Always some weird rustling from underneath the counter, but I never asked why, just clocked in and out. I wasn't trying to set pages on fire. I liked my life without a husband. Just me and my tree, climbing toward sun. Of course, the sunlight in my garage was artificial, because growing marijuana was illegal. Owning multiple guns was not. This didn't make me want to own guns; it made me wish that marijuana was legal and that my tree could flourish in the salty air, or at least by the window with a view of the sea.

My tree's solitude worried me. I had no evidence that it wanted solitude; basic facts of botany suggested otherwise. So I lugged a pink flowered armchair into my garage, and set up a reading light, and a table, and a basket of chocolate-covered pretzels. Early each morning and late at night I sat with my tree and read aloud. If I read from a graphic novel, I described each page in detail, to mix things up. The more I read to my tree, the faster it grew. I thought about naming it, crossing that line, but I knew if I did, I'd never love another man or woman again. I would end up married to a tree, a bonsai named Darby, Britta, or Snake.

DAPHNE

The thing about growing older is that you don't stop until you're dead, so you can't really compare it to anything in front of you. You can only compare backwards. Everyone thinks the old days were better; me, I remember the bad with the good. Like my first lover, first and last man who touched me. I was a Playboy Bunny back in the day, cocktail waitress, bunny ears tilted. Hef himself bit the tip of my left ear one night when he was angry. Sex softened him, made him go limp. He lay there while I hopped around, pawing sheets into a dirty den.

Hef didn't like to see us eat. He'd bring us three at a time to his room and watch us starve, hours and hours, until we bit and licked each other mostly from hunger. Now, in my cave under the desk, I eat toast with butter dripping down my chin.

He was never sure what we wanted, never quite confident that we weren't faking, and we faked it all the time, bunny ears dangling, jaundiced fur. Just once I thought about killing him, slitting his chest to see if his heart was beating. He was defensive about not getting it up. We folded into ourselves, each other. Lights flickered until morning when newspapers slid under the door, servants outside, underpaid and angry all the time. Sometimes we switched places, and sometimes we weren't sure who was blowing Hef and who was scrubbing shit from his toilet. Everything in the mansion existed to pleasure him. His greatest fear was being bored.

Once, exhausted after hours of no sleep, no food, rote positions, I asked him why he didn't read.

He looked startled, as if the thought hadn't occurred to him.

"You run a magazine," I said, "so read."

After that, ghost reader, I selected fiction for the magazine. I was the editor behind the editor behind the assistant behind the desk. I chose stories like this one, the story you're reading, between hunger and danger, yellow lamp of my bed.

GIRL IN PERFUME

THE FEAR HAD TO BE TAUGHT. It wasn't something women were born with. Kirstin birthed the fear in them, not like giving birth, but like controlling a robot.

It was Kirstin's job to make women think their body odors were bad. To scare them at the signature of their own scent, sour them on sweat, breath, sticky under the arms, wet between the legs. The product itself meant nothing. It was just scented water.

Kirstin had only been with SenX for a year when she realized that the company's research strategy wasn't working at all. Sure, Kirstin could try to create new online questionnaires, new clipboard quizzes. She could generate rich data, crunch numbers all day, but what was missing was the actual scent.

Kirstin herself didn't wear perfume. She was mildly allergic to scented products. Her hands were constantly red and itchy, but she stayed on at SenX because it paid so well. A job this glossy felt like a life. She had her own condo, 498 square feet in South Lake Union. Everything in her condo was unscented and spare.

After a year of what wasn't working, Kirstin pitched an idea to her boss. He held meetings on a treadmill desk or a trampoline; employees could pick. Kirstin chose the treadmill because when he talked to her from his tiny trampoline, she felt dizzy. Also, the perfume smell in the treadmill room was lighter, less cloying. It was a men's scent called "Take a Hike."

On the day of their meeting, her boss was on the treadmill when she arrived, running and talking into his phone.

"Hang on," he said into his cell. Then to Kirstin: "Whatcha got?"

"I believe that we need to move product development beyond data and into … "

"Okay," he said. Into his cell: "I'm back."

Kirstin waited for more, but there wasn't any. The next day a budget appeared on her desk: an insane amount of money with no agenda, no suggestions, no requirements. For research, wet signature illegible.

So Kirstin put up flyers to recruit test subjects, women between the ages of 25–42. The ages were random, chosen to give some semblance of signification. Test subjects were paid $1000 to live in a hotel for a week, doing nothing but eating, sleeping, watching TV, reading, talking, looking out the window, jogging in place and/or stretching, and talking on the landline. At night they slept piled together on the beds like puppies, but bigger and angrier, dreaming violent dreams.

The one condition of their participation was that they not bathe or brush their teeth or wash their faces or pluck hairs or cut nails or wipe themselves after using the toilet or engage in any form of personal hygiene whatsoever. For women with vaginas, tampons and pads were also forbidden, although Kirstin permitted highly absorbent period underwear after striking a deal with the underwear company to provide freebies in exchange for product placement.

To ensure compliance, Kirstin sat at the desk in the hotel room, reading magazines and eating the bottom, cakey part of cupcakes. She left the frosted tops of the cupcakes in a pile, which grew taller and taller until one of the test subjects (she never managed to learn their names) jogged past the icing tower and grabbed a handful, stuffing it into her mouth.

As required, all of the women tweeted, texted, Instagrammed, and otherwise boosted the signal. The pictures and captions they posted were cheerful, filled with jokes about how smelly they were, about how much fun they were having together. Like a giant slumber party. Like camp. Like a porno, test subjects fucking in the shower stall. Kirstin was fine with all of it. They'd signed the release. She figured SenX could use the video footage for their top secret scented virtual reality project.

Kirstin sat at the desk, reading magazines, eating cupcakes, texting and liking friends' posts on Facebook. She didn't need to pay attention because she had power over them; she was running the show. She left the room precisely at 5 p.m. and walked down the carpeted hallway to the elevator. Then she took the elevator to the 11th floor, where she got out and walked down the carpeted hallway to her room. Her room looked exactly like the test subjects' room. Inside she wiped, cut, scrubbed, and showered. She ordered dinner from room service and texted her fiancé, Chad.

The test subjects had been in the experimental trial for four days when the phone in Kirstin's room rang at 10:42 p.m. She wondered if room service had come back with dessert or more breadsticks.

"Hello?"

"Hello. This is the front desk. I'm afraid there's a disturbance on the 21st floor." The dial tone buzzed in her ear.

Kirstin groaned. Stepped out of her slippers, tugged off her pajamas, and squeezed back into her suit. Glancing in the mirror she realized she had bits of pizza smeared on her chin. She wiped with one of the bone white towels, gargled some mouthwash, and stepped into the hall.

The minute she stepped from her room into the hall, she could smell it. The smell sent her stumbling backwards, gasping, clawing at her door. Fumbling in her purse, she found the keycard and slid it into the slot. The light blinked red. Again. Red light.

Unable to go back, Kirstin pushed through the smell toward the elevator. Pressed L and waited while the doors shut with a whoosh. Then nothing. No movement. She tried 1 through 10. Crackling, the intercom voiced its displeasure. "Going up," the voice said, and then she was, elevator rising, numbers lighting and again going dim, all the way to 21.

On the 21st floor, the doors opened and the voice crackled.

"Get the fuck out," it said, and she did.

Here the scent was even stronger. Kirstin stood, silent and still, hands over her mouth, breathing through her nose, aware of her heels sinking into the carpet, aware that the door to room 2101 was wide open. She could hear ice clinking, soft hum of the soda machine, television blaring, the white noise of sleep. But wasn't this, she thought through the smell, exactly what her experiment was meant to capture? She had vials for this, jars and sticks in her purse.

Kirstin walked toward the open door, unlatching her purse, fumbling for the jars and sticky paper that was specially made to capture the smell. This was what she was born to do; it was her moment. She walked toward the room where she, Kirstin Jennifer Diffenbacher, would capture the pure, natural smell of the modern American woman (cis and/or trans). This smell would then be used to instill fear in women who would buy their products. And of course, in secret, it would be reproduced as part of the new artificial-reality scented porn films SenX had been developing for years.

Kirstin stepped toward the open door. Walked through the narrow hallway, then into the sitting room of the suite, where half a dozen people sat on the sofa and armchairs, white lab coats starched, paper masks over their mouths.

One of the men gestured for her to sit in a chair by the window. A woman took her arm and immediately Kirstin felt the needle sink below the skin.

"Beautiful work," someone said. The others nodded.

"You captured it," said the woman with the needle. "You smell exactly like fear in the context of meaningless control, mixed with corporate power undiluted by ethical standards. We're calling it *Mid-Level*. The bottle's tall, glass stopper."

Kirstin nodded, wondering if she'd get a raise, if she could refinance her condo, if Chad would propose.

GIRL IN TEMPERAMENTAL FABRIC

IN THE BEGINNING, when designers dressed us, we had to point to where our crack was. They kept turning us around, turning and turning, for men and women to look back there when they were making gowns of temperamental fabric.

We were only wearing short ivory smocks with little white slips.

How low is too low, they wanted to know.

"I don't want the crack showing," one said.

And he kept asking about my crack—the crack, the crack, the crack—but didn't even bother to ask our names.

"Is that your crack?" he asked. "Is this it? Is it here? Or here? Or there? Where does it start? Where does it end?"

I had to point to where my crack was, again and again, to show him how low was too low.

The temperamental fabric falling to pieces, he turned me around for the other designers also inquiring about my crack. And the cracks of the other girls, who were waiting.

The other girls stared at me. I stared back.

The designer said my crack would be a problem to solve, another issue he had to deal with in cutting and measuring such temperamental fabric for my gown.

He grabbed my elbow and spun me around.

I had to do it all over again, for him, long before he ever considered my eyes.

GIRL IN DEEP

My aunt always hated me, ever since I was a child. I never knew why, until she told me she was living in an ass crack with a bunch of women.

"I've lived in an ass crack since I was a child," she said, "because I'm female and no one wanted a girl like me, so I had to move into this ass crack with a bunch of women and make it into a home."

"You're so darn spoiled," she once told me. "You don't even deserve to live in an ass crack, and here you are living in a nice house with your family, as if you belong."

Even though she hated me, I really wanted to see where she lived, so I begged her to take me there.

"Are you sure?" she asked. "It's really tight. It's dark, and it kind of stinks in there, and sometimes there are weird noises. And once you get inside, certain people may not want you to ever leave."

GIRL IN CRACK

HELLO. ARE YOU THERE?
Is anyone out there?
We're inside the crack.
Calling to you, the answer is silence.
Until we hear each other's voices.
We're deep, deep inside the crack.
It stinks in here.
It really, really stinks.
Dark and damp, the crack is widening.

GIRL IN MEDICAL TRIALS[153]

THE SKELETONIZED WATCH RESEARCHERS building on each other's discoveries,[154] hoping for shorter hospital stays and longer life spans with less suffering.[155] Hope dims in the girl's eyes like dark areas[156] in a lightbox photograph. Is that Mommy? She asks. In the last days, she was afraid of me and didn't even know who I was. She couldn't recognize me, and I couldn't touch her.[157] Mommy, will we ever be able to come home? I was like, no.[158] It was as if all my childhood memories were gone, taken from me. Watching your best friend leaving is hard, but not as hard as watching yourself leaving.[159]

---

[153] She couldn't pay her rent, and they promised her more than donating plasma.

[154] Occasionally fighting over who gets credit for which sequence, which clot, which drop of blood.

[155] The insurance industry is fine with this, as long as fewer people have health insurance, so stats balance out.

[156] Islands or ghosts or alphabet suicides.

[157] This wasn't a symptom. This was the trial.

[158] Meaning "no" with a softening, a distance, a distraction built into the word, between "N" and "O," as if the word expanded. Never "yes."

[159] Payment came six months later, in the form of coupons for blockbuster film tickets and artificially buttered popcorn at the local mall.

When I participate in Girl in Maze,[160] everything they feed me fuels the runaround.[161]

I scramble, circling, smashing into walls.

Identical corners and corridors blind me, lure me back into the maze.

Sometimes it takes days to reach the stage.[162]

The stage is my destination, the only thing in the maze other than me. I can be in the maze, running, or I can be onstage.

Onstage, I give a little shake, do my dance, twirl, spread, and spin.[163] There's a pole, and I climb up until I reach the bucket.[164] I slide down using my thighs, one hand gripping the bucket. The food in the bucket is always the same: peanut butter and jelly on wheat, a banana, three carrots (including green tops), a half-empty vanilla blueberry yogurt, and a cheeseburger.[165] Every so often there's also an entire chocolate cake, complete with candles, which makes me think it's my birthday, or a special day for someone somewhere else.[166]

Sometimes I can't reach the food, because I'm stuck in the maze for days, racing around, wrong turn after wrong straight line. I can't find the stage, so I don't get fed.[167]

---

[160] This carnival ride, outlawed in the 1970s, was secretly reassembled at a clandestine asylum specializing in experimental treatment of female heroin addicts and alcoholics from prominent families. Women who come here are daughters, wives, and mothers of millionaires, even billionaires. The treatment is more powerful than an ice-pick lobotomy, and the women end up with improved figures due to Pavlovian recreation.

[161] Problematic patients are isolated in the runaround.

[162] Public humiliation is vital to this stage of treatment.

[163] This is the only way they will ever learn.

[164] Rehab is a bitch.

[165] There's a cheeseburger? Must be a mistake. No one authorized this.

[166] Cake is a delusion. Or possibly a wishful lie. Addicts are full of delusions.

[167] True.

Twice now, when I'd truly given up and fallen on the floor and thought I'd die from hunger and exhaustion, a voice sputtered out of a loudspeaker high on the wall.[168]

"Turn left," the voice said.

I crawled left.

"Turn right," the voice said, "and go straight and then go left again."

The first time I heard the voice, I thought maybe I was imagining it.[169] Then when I reached the stage, and danced, all wobbly and sick from hunger, and tried to climb the pole and fell, and waited for the bucket to descend on an invisible rope, which it didn't do, all I could think about was food.[170]

The second time I heard the voice, I tried to talk back.[171]

That didn't shake out too well.

Sometimes, randomly, the food stops.[172] Sometimes, randomly, I climb the pole and there's nothing there, so I slide down, start over, climb again, thighs raw, over and over until in anger I shake the pole as if the bucket might fall like fruit. When I give up, I sleep, curled tight, hungry, and when I wake, I'm lost again, maze closing in, running as if time might change the useless pattern of things.[173]

---

[168] Hi, there. Just so you know, you're not alone.

[169] The voice is real. The voice is me.

[170] Pavlov's dogs never get old here because our patients become Pavlov's dogs.

[171] Big mistake.

[172] Hunger is the greatest teacher.

[173] During the 1890s Russian physiologist Ivan Pavlov was looking at salivation in dogs in response to being fed, when he noticed that his dogs would begin to salivate whenever he entered the room, even when he was not bringing them food. Recreating the same response pattern in rehab, through the "Girl in Maze" trials, we combine the appropriate amount of disorientation and public humiliation to cure addiction. But some women are so fun to watch that we take our time releasing them, long after they are cured and the videos of their treatment are catalogued for study and sold to their families.

Now the girl in the dark[174] room says she remembers shivering, a fellow prisoner where you were with me, where she[175] was.

Before.

She's gone now, but you're here in the dark, whispering her name.

We touch, breast to breast, as if in grainy films from the 1970's.[176]

Old fantasies: vintage porn controlled and viewed by people[177] we can't see.

And wouldn't want to imagine.[178]

Although the idea of them is always with us.

The only rule where we are trapped is never to do it alone, never in private.

That's why we rush to the dark room.

In the glass house, even our most intimate moments must be put onstage, on display, consumed for the pleasure of others.

---

[174] The history of literature is filled with "dark this" and "dark that." Every bride is white. Every heroine is white and fragile. I want to live in this dark room, the opposite of white, the opposite of brides and fragile lilies, dark for safety, dark for privacy, dark for the one place we can be together as we wish we could be if it were safe to be visible in the harsh glare of white lights, white noise, and white lies.

[175] We gave each other names in the dark, kept them secret under our tongues.

[176] Such as: *Summer Trysts at Twisted Oak, Reminiscences of Bitter Oleander, Charmed Beach House Boudoir*

[177] Men, mostly, but occasionally women. These women work hard not to be us. They work hard to hold their bodies tight, upright, and dry. They never ooze, never shake their tits, only men's hands with a firm, tight grasp. They know their position is never secure. One slip, one drop of blood or exposed strap, and they might find themselves on the other side of the glass, among us, just like us.

[178] Imagination is the greatest weapon we have. We train ourselves to imagine resistance, rebellion, and riot; to imagine pleasures we choose and words we control; to imagine our bodies outside this glass house. Imagination is the dark room: not a place, but a belief. We call it hope.

Cameras are everywhere, hidden behind portraits, above doorways, in high corners, even in the showers and facing the toilets and beds.[179]

The doors have been removed from their hinges. The showers have transparent glass doors, no curtains, like the windows.

Our bodies are objects of art,[180] not personal but cultural, and therefore no longer our own.

Even as a young woman, I was made to feel at home on the shrine, the gynecological throne where my legs splayed for strangers to gaze inside me.

My ankles bound and spread wide, my feet hung in stirrups.

As I readied myself for the speculum and the bimanual examination, they told me to relax.[181]

---

[179] Why are you surprised by this? Why do you read this as fiction? You were warned. You were groomed by reality TV, by pop-up ads in search engines that read your mind, by the NSA, by the 2016 election to expect that every corner held the camera's eye, and every move, word, touch was simultaneously experienced and recorded. You were slowly trained to disengage from the idea of privacy, to leave privacy behind like childish things. Like dolls.

[180] Art desires only to exist outside the marketplace, to exist as value in and of itself. But there is no outside. We are all inside the marketplace. And so beauty and desire and even love all come with a price.

[181] "You look cute when you're angry."

GIRL IN INTELLIGENCE TEST

THIS TEST DISTINGUISHES different levels of intelligence among female subjects from a diverse range of socioeconomic backgrounds. While the test has long been accused of bias, since it was designed by a group of highly influential males worried about false accusation, Problems 4 & 5 have been eerily precise in predicting which subjects will go on to marry well.

Here are five problems taken from the female intelligence test, followed by an Answer Key.

Problem 1 requires you to find the odd girl out.

Problems 2 and 3 require you to find the intoxicated girl, among six tipsy adult women, legally able to consent to slam dunking water balloons. (Hint: one of the girls remains intact despite her inability to hold her liquor.)

Each girl has three types of interchangeable heads, bodies, legs, and hips in each row. The mystery girl has round, white breasts, a thin waist, and long thin legs.

Intact water balloons, among natural water-balloon virgins and reborn water-balloon virgins, aim to measure six main abilities prized by pop culture: choosing, filling, throwing, perpetuating myths (most rapes don't occur in dark alleys), turning rapists into victims, and trivializing sexual violence.

Since the test consists of a series of problems degraded according to their relative difficulty, Problems 4 & 5 are a bitch, literally and metaphorically. These two bitches are more effectively administered in terms of an individual's position in each group, preferably by a subject from a group of bitches representing a population of bitches to which she belongs.

GIRL IN NUDE

DOLLHOUSE WINDOWS curtained a fog of unknowability
    White-sand beaches, private,
    She would have followed him anywhere, even into the
    Black car with tinted windows, the one that drove her to
the dollhouse,
    In the black car, for an audience of one, she'll remember
    A senior in high school, in the apartment building, a boy
walked out from the shadows, as if it were just an accident, but
later she realized
    She followed him, leaving her family to create another life,
    To get to know him, as a couple, a new family as alterna-
tive reality
    In a theater home of a dramaturge, a place for girls
    Go live in captivity, in a life-sized dollhouse,
    Occasionally, he said, "They would be allowed to walk on
leashes in the sun, but only if
    The food she ate with her handlers:
    The dollhouse served impeccable, unforgettable cuisine,
but what surprised her was
    The black car with tinted windows, the one that took her
to the dollhouse,

102

Where she followed him, never realizing he was also a girl, a girl, whose name was

The director of the collection she once thought was a boy, the one who had taken off her leashes in the sun,

With short hair, this person she loved now realized she didn't know,

While standing on the platform near the golden piano,

Singing soprano as if summoning a demon that would follow all motions inside a Disneyland without children,

When the board voted to include you in the collection,

When he introduced her behind a one-way glass wall, a mirror

Reflecting your own nakedness,

Philanthropic collectors of girls

Former administrators of the collection now in charge of the dollhouse endowment

Only dream of the Girl Zoo

A black car marring white-sand beaches

GIRL IN SPECIAL COLLECTOR'S EDITION

IF SHE'S A STACKED BLONDE like her dead mother, she needs city lights' iconography in careful stiletto steps inching towards a man who will be her benefactor or her murderer. Like the police, she forgets to care.

Before she realizes he is making her dreams comes true, he promises to put her in the special collector's edition, mapped out on the screening-room floor. In the dark, his powerful hands travel over her body, after a mickey, another blackout where the last thing she sees are his smiling eyes and remembers the accident, how her mother died at the window factory infused with light.

Her mother was the girl in the window. Then, the window broke and she was gone, instantly, one part of her body severed from another by the window that trapped her.

Like the witness of a freak accident wearing Candy perfume, she recalls odd things, making bizarre connections, like the way sexual dependency smells like a Prada handbag dropped onto an unmade bed. Her heroes are thieves, men and women brave enough to steal a girl from her life. Few are willing to steal the ones giving themselves away.

Even while getting high, she avoids tattoos until an inventive and demanding casting director convinces her to have a permanent garter etched high on her delicate thigh. After the tattoo, she cries elegantly, and he takes photographs.

The tattoo throbbing, she falls asleep in a brick-walled bedroom on a stained mattress heaped with clothing of women she doesn't know.

On the brick wall are acrylic portraits of smiling dogs painted by an amateur artist with no talent, yet the eyes are so beautiful, like her mother's eyes painted with liquid liner in the style of Cleopatra. The artist is here, not speaking, just painting the dogs' eyes, again and again, in the portraits. He paints them with layers and layers of liquid eyeliner stolen from her makeup bag.

She rises from the bed, covered in sweat, and wants to take a bath but finds the blue bathroom with its vintage clawfoot tub is full of video cameras, green lights blinking in the high corners of the ceiling. She wants to cry, again, but stops, remembering her presence, what her eyes look like with streaked mascara and thinks this might be her chance to recreate herself in another's eyes, for a stranger to record the details of what happens.

She bathes, gazing into the camera while lathering her hips and thighs with pink soap, taking special care with the tender tattoo.

Healing in bloody bands, she remembers growing up in a house full of dogs in Lexington, where her father sang ballads to her mother all through the night. But after her mother died, she witnessed the last days of her childhood when the dogs were sent away, her father stopped singing, and the world became dark until she began to lighten, strangely, from within.

GIRL IN STAIRS

SOMETIMES CHILDREN TUMBLE down into stairs.

Ascending the stairs, a child plummets like a star in charcoal.

A tiny want to descend, a child falls in.

One step folding in on itself like a petal creates a narrow door where a child will fall.

A child plummets into the stairs where an old man sits on a chair, alone, in darkness, waiting.

Down into the darkness.

Flailing on the floor in the charcoal room hidden inside the stairs, inside the wooden stairs, a girl navigates the narrow closet like a sawdust hallway without openings, hoping to crawl into other rooms.

In the dark, inside the stairs, in the room with no exit, she wakes on the wooden floor, the bare and dusty wood.

Coughing and crying, though awake, she feels as if she has been sleeping.

Her eyes adjust to darkness.

A single light comes on, one light only, one tiny light on a chain, dangling above so she can see the room inside the stairs is spare and the light shines on dust, flitting in waves on air.

She weeps and tries to stand for the man sitting on the chair in the corner. He's smiling. She waves. He comes near, leaning over so she sees his charcoal eyes, the color of darkness, when he explains how he plummeted as a child, long ago.

GIRL IN BUNK

EASY TO WARN THE GIRL in the slasher pic with a hiss and a shudder. Easy to sentence her to death, dismemberment at Bible camp, where you go to ride bareback and braid doormats from bread bags. Your counselor is tall, blonde Sally, and tan. Later at dance camp, you flail on your toes. At cheerleading camp, you wear a short skirt that sways when you walk, as if someone's watching. Someone is always watching a girl. Listen carefully to the ghost in the movie. The ghost in the movie made unfortunate choices, which you never do. She's nothing like you. And now she's nothing, blank bed in your cabin, where you rest after Crafts while you count down to Pool. She's so gone it's wholesome: purse on a hook, copper penny missing where good luck lurks.

GIRL IN CAVITY

MY SKULL REMAINED INTACT long after the rest of my body had decayed.

Now, it's a house for a little, tiny girl, who builds a nest inside bones which once housed my brain.

She has two twin swing sets—each a little porch swing hanging inside the cavity of my eyes.

My teeth are bridges.

GIRL IN GLASS

TAKE ME OUT. Play with me. I'm shivering. You can flip the switch to make shadows go. I shudder, waiting to roam. The glass fills with light. Piped-in air smells of candy, girls trembling after misted showers spritz us with moisturized, perfumed waters. Hot air vents blow-dry our faces, hair, and bodies, coated in gleaming oils and aloe. After the shower, we are lonely, even for each other. Each isolated in our own parallel cube, we are displayed, stacked beside, below, and above other nude girls encased in this giant rectangle of glass walls. The case shimmers. I stare out at the dollhouse and shudder. The glass case quakes. Girls quiver. When the floor becomes a treadmill, we run in our cubicles, exercising for hours like hamsters in a cage so our muscles will not atrophy. When the showers mist us, again, all our sweat and tears go down the drain. Clean, perfumed, glistening flesh behind gleaming glass, we are curiosities, living dolls, shadows or light. We are ready to live again. Outside the glass, the dollhouse beckons full of wonderful toys—the kitchen with its sinks, pots, dishes, and ovens. All the curiosities in cabinets. Toilets! The tufted bathroom matts so pastel like after-dinner mints shattered by pestles. Oh, I love toilets! There's nothing greater than toilets. I love to shit on them and shit on them. It feels so good, even when I know you're watching from

110

the peephole. All the halls! The halls, the halls, the halls, the halls, the halls where we can walk again. The bedrooms where we can sleep in beds! I almost remember what it's like to drink real water from a glass, to touch curtains, to sing with other girls. Even if it hurts, it feels good to hunger, for the stomach and organs to really awaken, free from feeding tubes, catheters, and colostomy bags. All these clear tubes dripping in and out of me, tying me down, binding me to the case. I want to be able to move. I would love to move my bowels when I decide. I would rather be owned than forgotten. I would rather be used than thrown away. I like to shit on toilets and to bathe in bathtubs. I like to drink water from glasses and to eat food I can chew and swallow and put into my mouth, even if someone else is playing with me, deciding what food to put in the house to trap me like a mouse. I'll take the bait. Make me do anything. I just want to be chosen. Please, please take me out. I will be good. I promise. I will do anything, anything you want. Anything at all. I promise we will have fun, if you just open the glass case. You'll see why I am better than the other dolls in the collection. Oh, the things I will do. The things you can do to me. I love you. I love you. I do. I'm yours. I will be yours and you will be mine. Put me in any room and tell me what to do. I'll play all day. Just give me a chance to get out. Let me out. The glass is breaking. It shatters me inside where the doll clothed in light is full of darkness as the peppermint air flows through vents with laughing gas. Now, comes the music. Beethoven, as usual. We are all laughing. Even though we can't hear each other, we see everything. I see the other girls. They see me. It's funny, so funny, even though I don't remember why and will likely start crying again at any moment, for reasons unknown.

GIRL IN HALFWAY HOUSE

IF THE NAKED OLD MAN on the sofa is not your grandfather, let's pretend he's mine. Try not to wake him. He's sleeping, so he can't be blamed for the black worms in the shower. They'll turn into drain flies soon and will fly away. Besides, the black worms are the only pets he can keep. When the sink won't drain, just reuse the water. Gray water is still good water, even if it's not clear. If the toilet won't flush, don't tell anyone, especially if it overflows. No one wants to know. The drain flies will devour anything floating in stagnant water.

It's rude to speak of the toilet.

Let's pretend the toilet doesn't exist.

Now, let's pretend the old man isn't here. His penis is a flower. A rare and beautiful flower unlike any flower you've ever seen.

GIRL IN DRAIN

To: Curator, Glass Uprising Exhibit
From: Museum of Late American Artifacts
RE: GIRL IN DRAIN

I[182] did not see rain for the first sixteen[183] years of my life, but at the hospital I saw old dolls like me discarded down the drainage system where the blood[184] goes smoothly because there is no dissent.

Long ago, skipping[185] through the trauma ward, I learned how to fake a ruptured hymen and an orgasm with an unwashed finger in the wound.

Once the blood comes, a girl's useful life as a plaything[186] is over, but she is allowed to see rain.

Old dolls like me are never played with and are only used to make other dolls with their bodies with doctors, lawyers,

---

[182] Subject was permitted to keep a diary, which has been translated from Girlspeak by both human and computer Girlspeak authorities. This translation is the definitive edition.

[183] Subject's time-based age unknown.

[184] Not to be spoken of.

[185] In late American culture, prior to The Glass Uprising, skipping was considered a sign of heightened emotion.

[186] There is no precise word for "plaything." In the original document, the word is a pun involving both blood oranges and bocce.

CEOs, priests, princes, and learned men who wear jade masks[187] in the sugar room.

When I was no longer fit to be a maker, I became a rain walker.

Paid sixty-five dollars[188] a month, I never got a raise or a pension, no matter how many times I conceived. But when thunder rolled, I could traipse through the dampened cemetery[189] with other makers and rain walkers who chose to buy a plot with their monthly wages so diggers[190] could make a hole to house the old body.

We were just hoping to escape the drain, didn't want to be processed into sludge with the ones who gave up, the ones who couldn't earn enough[191] to buy a room of their own on this little plot of land, an underground room, six feet under.

Every other old doll, she just wanted a room like me, knowing she was too old to be a plaything and would have to find a place for herself without being displayed in another's room.

No longer fit to display in the glass case, once I became

---

[187] Here the subject reveals her blatant hostility toward men, especially men in masks made of ornamental materials.

[188] Dollars were translated into pennies and pennies translated into sexual favors; see "coin of the realm."

[189] Cemeteries figured prominently in late American death mythology.

[190] Debate continues between human and computer translators regarding the word "diggers." The computer translators believe that the word refers to "liking" something – "I dig blood sports," for example. The human translators believe that the word refers to gravediggers – "I have to dig three graves before lunch."

[191] Here, subject seems to set herself above or against the others, which is a common theme in diary texts from this time, and merits further study as we continue to pinpoint the authentic beginnings of the uprising, and the figures central to its outcome.

damaged, I refused to be deranged,[192] realizing I could ruin naturally by taking walks in the rain.

I just wanted to sleep peacefully in my coffin,[193] where no one could bother me or watch me as I closed my eyes. That was my reward, that my body would finally be hidden. All I wanted was to pay for my grave, until I was sixteen and tasted rain. Then, I wanted the soft cool drops falling on my tongue and face forever.[194] [195]

---

[192] This poetic repetition of sounds is computer generated, and not present in the original text.

[193] Similar to a breadbox, but housing death. Both were often made of wood.

[194] Note the subject's nostalgia for the natural world, and the fantasy of taste.

[195] In late American mythology, the number thirteen was considered unlucky. Hotels often deleted the thirteenth floor from the record, implying that twelve was twelve, but fourteen was thirteen, and fifteen was fourteen, and so on. However, new research reveals a vast conspiracy among hotel owners involving the thirteenth floor. Every thirteenth floor remained intact, but inaccessible by the usual methods (elevator, stairs). The floor was windowless, accessible only by retinal identification. Dollhouses were built in these liminal, unlucky spaces, and girls were kept stacked in glass boxes, for use as their functions dictated.

GIRL IN ELECTRIC CHAIR

FOUR STACKED TENEMENT ROOMS, two bathrooms, plugs, sockets, bare bulbs, and then the face peeking through the hole with transparent frame: I finally discovered, at the hardware store, materials to build the chair that will be used to electrocute me.

Setting the stage with tape wiring in the mini sockets, the little girl asked me if I was going to be electrocuted and if I understood how the hole worked.

I had been staring at her through the lens box by the light of gel-colored bulbs. She had decided she wanted me to go au naturel when she began to shock me with the Taser mounted in the celling.

She was a child, just a child. I kept reminding myself. I was the adult, a grown woman. That was why she enjoyed doing this to me.

Shocking adults, why is it so much fun? The clhild asked, and children would do it all the time, given the opportunity. There would be much money to be made in this new game, if only I could find a way to patent it. But why, why was it so much fun?

I didn't know what to tell the girl, which was sad for me, since I am the inventor. Parents have long asked the question of why. I was one of the designers of the original special collector's edition Electric-Chair Barbie, and this is what inspired me to create the toy, Girl in Electric Chair. I was more than delighted to discover affluent girls like her would be happy to purchase poor women like me from an online store with things to make such wonderful toys.

One day I will build a tiny casket for her to bury me after burning me alive, but for now she will have to hide me in the hole, to take a break from my shock therapy in this game that trains her to be mine.

Next, I will create a toy version of The Old Woman in the Shoe, but I must be careful because the woman has many welfare children and no two people's teeth are exactly alike. Most of the witnesses to her disappearance have either disappeared or died, and I have hoarded the old brown shoes the woman was wearing along with neighborhood rumors that said I would have to face the electric chair if caught.

GIRL IN FINGER WEB

I WAS IN A WEB OF FINGERS obscuring the warehouse where girls were kept in boxes like the one I escaped. Sister lullaby singing swallowed this closeness, so male, the other body, the boy's hand sliding across her belly, the beauty of him, not the beauty of women and girls at the abandoned warehouse where we sat with the body I thought was like the statue of David. But I kept remembering skin scratched with splinters and mites. I dug and pried. Broke my nails, fingers torn to shreds. When a board finally gave, I pulled, busted a hole, a hollow for me to wriggle, breasts and back scraping wet concrete.

It took a while before I could see again.

Narrow crumbling concrete halls, blood on walls, I stumble. Her hands cover my eyes. Hers with others. Soon, I'm in a web of fingers obscuring, rough with dried blood—light from dusty barred windows, crates stacked on crates. Outside, sunlight, blinding white, erases the trees as birds sing to the river of the warehouse, where girls are kept in boxes like the one I escaped, sister lullaby singing.

GIRL IN LIGHTHOUSE

COME WITH ME TO THE LIGHTHOUSE, and we'll eat she-crab soup. Watching the tail of a whale—a humpback vanishing into blue waters—we'll share our home with peregrine falcons as we cuddle and shiver at the watcher's windows, light combing dark sea. For centuries, women like us have searched for shipwrecks, our eyes weaving over water, all night, every night, waiting for sailors to shore. Our ancestors were women who loved ancient mariners and hoped to save them when they failed to return. The voyage is the destination, the sea a grave lost to waters that feed us, nursing our bodies, even our dreams.

In the lighthouse, I whisper, but you are so afraid, hiding in the dark, as if you don't want me to see your face, though we were once closer than sisters. You are afraid because people have lied about the way we jumped off the bridge. People have been saying we drowned. I had to hide when I couldn't go back, couldn't risk the police knowing I live in the lighthouse now, squatting, lonely, ever since friends said I was swimming with you naked in the dark, the sea cooling our legs tangling in the warmth of our bodies, yours opening to mine as we were sinking, pulling each other under.

"Don't," you said as I started to swim, "stop."

I said, "We're going to drown."

As the searchlight of the lighthouse bobbed, you kissed me, and we swam where people told us not to, a place people said was dangerous. At night the dark waters, the paleness of your skin in moonlight, your eyes bright as you clutched me. Then, darkness. Nothing.

I wished you would never let go.

Please, don't leave me in the lighthouse, the creamy stone walls with cracked mortar, glowing fleshy by candlelight. I make soup from what the sea gives and watch for you in the windows. As the soup simmers, I smell tender cooked white fish and brine, tiny sand crabs bursting as I slowly sip and slurp from old pottery, uneven bowls made by the lighthouse keeper, your father, when he was a young man, too young to imagine bowls the color of the sea in the morning, just before a storm, a touch of green threaded into gray.

I have eaten turtle and starfish. I have eaten moss and crabs. Squid. And creatures that have no name. I have eaten the soup the sea gives when the sailor comes to tell me you have drowned. I don't want him to know who I am. He is tall with reddish-black hair and a ginger beard, so his leathery face seems cushioned by a lion's mane.

"I'll call you Feather," he says, "because your hair is like ravens' wings."

I close my eyes as he strokes my face, his calloused hands on my neck.

"You're so thin," he says, his fingers playing over my lips and clavicles. "Do you have anything to eat?"

I offer him the broth of steaming starfish, which he spoons into his bright red lips, kissed by the sun.

"Delicious," he whispers, finding a pregnant seahorse in his bowl.

He smiles while eating, the sea a mystery, feeding us then drowning us when we go too far into its waters.

GIRLS IN WAVES

1. *Girl in Waterbed:* Beneath you in waves, caressing, I scissor water holding you from above. You weigh me down. Waves shiver as you rise. An ocean of sleep, I'm the water you rest upon. I miss you, I miss you, when you don't come home. As you sleep, I wake. As you wake to leave me, I sleep.

2. *Girl in Garden:* Beneath dirt, iris roots grow through my tibia. Seeds of roses tangling on my ribs, rain falls into my gnawed ovaries, wilted, soaking the dark earth into my pelvis. In waves. I'm one with the flowers, decaying labia feeding vine. The zookeeper thinks he has hidden me to protect him, but I am protected, finally safe to sleep, my brain and uterus concealed with the morning glories to keep me company. No one will ever find me or any part of me: my vagina, hands, face, broken neck, and severed head a home to gentle worms, whose blind innocence touches me more gently than any living woman could ever imagine. Decay is heaven in the zookeeper's garden. After what I've gone through in the Girl Zoo, the garden is all I want. Once dismembered, dissected, and displayed in livestream vivisection, I am now concealed, though strangers see my beauty rise every spring in petals blooming. I'm safe here, where no

one can know what happened, why he put me here. Days of torture I have slowly endured and mostly forgotten, but I remember rooms I used to walk through with Mother's laughter coming in waves.

3. *Girl in the Curtain:* There are lots of carousel horses here and other carousel animals from the 1900s, antiques from the rise of the American zoo, when artists observed exotic animals up close in their cages and used these sketches to make carousel animals for children to ride. Some people say it's the same here in the Girl Zoo. Artists come to sketch us in our cages so they can design carousel women for people to ride. Visitors will ride these women carousels before and after viewing our exhibits. That's why I hide behind this curtain's velvet waves, to conceal my body from artists who want to sketch me.

4. *Girl in YouTube:* Thanks for checking out this video of the Girl Zoo. Be sure to subscribe because I upload a new girl every Thursday. Next Thursday will be the girl in the sea cave.

5. *Girl in the Sea Cave:* In the sea cave, captured by fishermen, you could have died as the mermaid's unblinking eyes stare back at you. Whatever is making that noise isn't supposed to be hiding here with you. The dead mermaid's face is growing too familiar, weirdly smiling as its right hand seems to be moving slowly toward a blinking light, a camera pointing at you. Of all the people you could be trapped with, it has to be your mother. And this is the dumbest stunt she has ever tried to pull to teach you to stand up for yourself, alleg-

edly to learn from what she has overcome. Out of the darkness, you see her delicate face, pale, demented as she swings the camera. This is what she finds: Screams! Running, you remember when you were a child, after your mother's kidnapping at sea, when the men caged her in tanks of water and told her she was a mermaid, ordering her into scuba gear to perform for the cameras inside the waterbed of the aquatic exhibit at the Girl Zoo. After her escape, when her doctors said the Girl Zoo wasn't real, they told you that you couldn't touch her because she was being treated with electroconvulsive therapy, small electric currents passing through her brain to trigger brief seizures to relieve depression. It worked only too well. Now, she has a happy resting face, like a lunatic gathering delight in the mundane, just as she seems to gather delight in your terror, perhaps thinking it a memory of her own.

6. *Girl in Contest:* Pay attention to the dark hole on the left. You can't hide forever. You can lose everything, hiding too long. You'll never be the same as you were before you were raped, but you could be even better, if you win the contest by figuring out a way to escape, before he attacks again. Don't let the rapist win! There's nothing more terrifying to him than a survivor, a living witness to tell the story, even if the story makes very little sense and ends up being about Girl Zoos and carousels of women and decaying mermaids. Listen, you're winning, just by breathing, by running, or at least finally getting far enough ahead of him to say: *Mother, wake up. Mother, can you hear me? You're not a decayed mermaid rotting in wet sand.* A washed-up creature, I gather you near, holding you until night falls, covering our nakedness with

an indigo blanket of life-sustaining terror knitted in a man's shadow.

GIRL IN THE MALL

NOTHING TO DO IN THIS TOWN but hang out at the mall. We buy pretzels and talk about school shootings, try on earrings, poking them in and everything. Which you're not supposed to do. Because germs. And try on bathing suits without underwear, which you're not supposed to do either. Because AIDS. You can get pregnant too. Which we are. Not from a bathing suit, but from John, who stuck his dick in Chrissy and then in me and told us not to tell. Now we're both pregnant by John, but you'd never know it because we're skinny like supermodels.

We go to the dressing room to try on thongs and give birth. "It's time," Chrissy says, so we bend over and babies come out. We wad them up with the clothes we don't buy. They're so shiny with gunk. They smell.

We take off our shirts and bras and make our boobs squish together.

"Maybe we're gay for each other."

"Nah," I say, thinking about John.

"But what if we are?"

"You're gay for me, but I'm not gay for you."

Chrissy punches me in the stomach and I fake like it hurts. Then we're on the floor laughing so hard we scare the dressing room girl, who knocks.

126

"Are you okay are you okay are you okay."

Chrissy pokes out her head. "Do you have this in size twelve?"

Before the dressing room girl comes back we stuff things down our pants. We leave our babies on the bench, oozing. Walk out slowly like we're totally chill.

In the parking lot all the cars look the same. My mom's car is white, four door, and she doesn't know I took it. We spend twenty minutes beeping the remote, waiting for a door to unlock.

"Did you like it?" Chrissy asks. I'm driving and she's cutting tags off our loot.

"Like what?"

"His dick in your pussy."

I have to think. "Sort of. I mean, I didn't come but it was warm and made me feel full."

"Sex makes me feel empty."

"You're gay, Chrissy. You don't like dick."

"I might like dick. I just don't like John."

I thought about the girl down the street who got abducted and then escaped a year later, with weird tattoos on her arms and dead eyes. Her name was Patti but he changed her name to Elysian Fields and now she went by Sian.

"Chrissy, do you ever talk to Sian?"

"You mean Patti?"

"I mean Elysian Fields."

"Not since he returned her."

"He didn't return her; she escaped. Hey, if someone abducts me, will you try to find me? Or will you forget and not want to look?"

Chrissy paused. "Realistically speaking? I mean, do you want a true answer?"

"Yeah. The truth."

"Of course I'd look for you. I'd never stop looking. But the truth is, if you go away for a year, I'm getting a new best friend."

"I'm your best friend?"

"Of course you are, dummy."

I didn't know whether to be happy that we were best friends or sad that I could be so easily replaced.

Mom tells me I could never be replaced because I'm an only child, but Mom hates malls, so I lie to her, never telling where I'm going with Chrissy, or what John has done.

When Mom was young, she worked in a record store in the same mall, a part-time employee with other teenage girls. When she and the other girls were working, a man would call the store and ask if they were on their period. The girls felt constantly watched, in danger, and kept calling mall security to walk them to their cars at night after closing, until it was discovered the calls were coming from the security office.

"What happened to me was nothing," Mom said. "Other girls lost everything in the mall, even their lives."

"Come on, Mom."

"How bad do you want to go shopping there? Is hanging out at the mall worth your future? Is it because of Chrissy, or some boy?"

"No," I lie.

"A man? Oh, god no, not a man!"

"No," I say, never daring to tell her about John or that he works as a mall security guard, her worst nightmare.

With Mom, mall horror stories never end. She makes no distinction between malls and haunted houses, except to say malls are more dangerous for girls to visit.

Every Christmas, instead of telling me the story of Christ's birth, she tells me the story of her childhood friends, Rachel Arnold Trlica, Renee Wilson, and Julie Ann Moseley who were seventeen, fourteen, and nine the last they were ever seen on December 23, 1974, when the three girls went to a Texas mall to do some last-minute Christmas shopping. All these decades later, they still have not returned.

"How awful," I whisper, holding Mom's hand while secretly planning another trip to the mall.

Later, I tell John what Mom said, and he laughs. "Those girls were taken from the Sears lot," he says. "I remember when it happened. The other mall security guards used to visit them all the time. They grew up in captivity in the Dallas–Fort Worth area, in the same town their parents were. By the time they were adults, they were members of the stable. The younger girl died giving birth to a child."

"Prove it," I say, thinking he's a liar.

"What?"

"Take me there."

"Where?"

"The stable."

"You?"

"I want to see it."

We get into his Honda, the one with tinted windows, and I'm surprised when he drives us back to the mall.

"Where are you taking me?" I ask.

"I thought you wanted to see it?"

It has been dark for hours, and the mall is closed. We wait in his car as security guards clear out the mall's halls, locking down the stores when John whispers: "In any mall, if a window looks like a mirror to you, people inside can see just fine."

"What people?" I ask.

"The ones in the stable."

Deep inside the empty mall, he leads me into places I never knew existed, secret tunnels security guards walk, the ones behind the girls' bathrooms, where mirrors are windows for men to look inside and the ceiling tiles and walls have peepholes. These tunnels eventually lead to the basement, where concrete floors have been hosed down near cages made of cyclone fencing with padlocks.

Girls' names have been scratched into the walls, carved crudely behind the cages along with beginning and end dates and scrawled trees with branches leading from the girls' names to the names of their children, born in captivity.

I imagine Mom's heart breaking when John informs me I'm not allowed to leave unless I can convince Chrissy to come here to take my place.

Days have turned to weeks as I wait.

Every day, I watch from behind the bathroom mirrors, waiting for Chrissy, thinking of ways to get her down here, as I plot my escape.

GIRL IN HAIRCUT

THERE WAS A TIME in early childhood when my sister and I were told we were no longer female. We were referred to as brothers, not sisters, not allowed to use the girls' bathroom or to stand in line with the other girls at school. Men we didn't know began to call us "sonny."

This was southern Oklahoma in the early 1980's. No one was talking about gender dysphoria, not alone its opposite, which my sister and I were suffering from, even though we were cis girls, female at birth.

For reasons beyond our control, we were suddenly treated like boys by society and didn't know how to respond, so we said nothing, being confused and ashamed when we were referred to as "he" or "him," not "she" or "her."

At school, the girls didn't want to hang out with us. Neither did the boys. It was a problem at the beginning of every school year and every time we had a substitute teacher. In music class, I was embarrassed during certain musical games, songs that required volunteers be separated by gender.

"Now, I need a girl. A girl to sing!" the new music teacher called out to my class of eager first graders. Having been passed over numerous times and wanting to sing, I desperately

131

raised my hand, wanting the teacher to choose me, only to be crushed when she gave me an annoyed look and said, "No, get your hand down! Not you. I said a girl. A girl! Not a boy!"

It was a problem at restaurants and gas stations, wherever we might need to use a public restroom. My sister was only four years old when she needed to go to the bathroom at a local Quik Mart and Mother told me to go with her. I was five or six at the time. I followed my little sister down a back hallway toward the restrooms, out of sight of Mother, only to watch in horror as an old man began to lure my sister away at the door of the Women's Room. He touched her arm, leading her away with him, saying, "No, no, come on, sonny, over here. Don't go in there, son. You're supposed to go in here." He led her inside the Men's Room, going in with her, closing the door.

Of course, we never told Mother, who kept insisting we get mushroom haircuts every other month, which I hated because I feared it made my sister and I look like boys, even though Mother assured us it didn't.

GIRL IN THE SILENT ROOM[196]

SINCE HER FATHER WAS AN ADDICT who could be cured in the silent room, she drew in blood images from her own life, especially childhood.[197]

She used her mom a lot—pale, anemic, the white space.[198]

In the garden of lilies, her mother's grubby hands unearthed the manhandled whose obsessions the women knew on days he could get the girl, how her thighs closed on the night. Hands caked with earth and blood, she whispered, "I was once in the silent room."[199]

Coming out of the woodwork, the blood people found us. Her hand hemorrhaging in the morning, her head wound healed through abscess, her thigh torn, septic, moistened by earth in the wound, soft parts to femur, the girl was making motions as if to indicate her blood[200] was paint.[201] She was painting in blood.

---

[196] Made for TV movie title: "Hometown Daughters: The Sequel"

[197] Product placement: doll in schoolgirl skirt

[198] Product placement: tooth whitener

[199] Product placement: meds (social anxiety, depression)

[200] Product placement: bleached cotton pads with stay-dry liner

[201] Product placement: Colonial Breezes interior paint palette colors for Spring

GIRL IN WHITE[202] WASHED WORLD

WOMEN WITH CHILDREN in state prisons[203] explore the language of poetry through neglect by association, finding poetry everywhere, even in each other's eyes, asking what is this poem asking of me?[204] They feed poetry, but it never feeds their daughters.[205] Even as you're waiting for her release,[206] watching at visiting hours from a distance, you're listening for the girl in this collection of women's voices married[207] to mishap

---

[202] Notice how the word breaks one story in two. "Girl in White" and "Girl Washed," maybe "Girlwash" like "Carwash" or "Girl, Washed Out," or "Watched," but missing *S* and subbing in *TC,* the sound they make when they want to say "less than."

[203] Deliberately ambiguous. Might mean: Women in state prisons who have children back home. Might mean: Women whose children are imprisoned by the state. Might mean: Women who are in prison and have children who are also in prison. Might mean: Lots of women locked up.

[204] To put the poem first is freedom.

[205] Their daughters go to the store and come home with empty paper bags. They live on air, which costs less than the bag.

[206] The word "release" feels bound to pleasure rather than justice. It feels like excess, like sunshine and orgasm and wine, like something given as a gift. But "release" here just means beginning again the lease you left behind, beginning again to live within the thing you borrowed, something you'll pay for in the end.

[207] Shadow overhead: expensive divorce.

and loss. Though you know better, you're optimistic[208] about your daughter returning home to a whitewashed world where hand-me-down songs are coming straight from the heart.

---

[208] Optimism is the opposite of knowledge. It's the thing that cancels out knowing, leaving room for fantasy. It's the net under the bridge that keeps you from jumping.

GIRL IN WOMAN[209]

Once the first girl falls[210] pregnant, if she sees the state of her body as the tyranny of beauty, the Cashmere Bouquet and the Dreamflower Box are the reasons for the eyebrow floating in the toilet with belladonna and mouse skin.

If she is lost to the new girl growing inside her, she will become her own mother, host to another life, and the reason why virgins with painted-on veins apply layers of liquid mascara with spiral brushes, carefully, artfully, an act of worship to secretly enhance their chances of transforming.

The outline of the virgin's eyes is an outcry for insemination, along with bee[211]-stung lips, the half-moons of manicure, those artificial fingernails not claw-like weapons for protection, but like a peacock's feathers, an invitation for mating, obscuring her humanity like wedding attire where the bride loves the sense of mystery created by the veil, hiding her eyes to emphasize the way her lips have become another labia,[212]

---

[209] Alternative spellings of "woman" typically accompany periods of social upheaval. The spelling of "girl" remains standard.

[210] From a great height, as when a girl is pushed off a roof after losing her virginity.

[211] Reference to "bees" dates this piece to the era of Environmental Collapse.

[212] Oh, sweetheart, calm down.

welcoming the male,[213] with lips painted pink or red or slath-
ered with glittery liquid gloss as if swollen and dripping with
moisture.

---

[213] Mail is also welcome, especially child support checks and coupons for milk.

GIRL ON TONGUE

WE'RE WAITING FOR ICE CREAM at a fancy shop. I'm maple; Rachel's chocolate mint. Local bands pulse from invisible speakers. A man shoves inside, girlfriend on tiptoe. They linger over flavors as the line snakes to the street.

Balsamic reduction's my favorite flavor, but not on maple. I choose almonds hidden inside. The idea is to walk and eat ice cream at the same time, a pleasure sweet because walking is sweet, and because of sun, rare in our city. Rachel and I trade flavors. "I'll try yours and you try mine."

The man who lingered wraps his arm around his girlfriend's waist. "I'll watch."

All four of us wait for the streetlight.

There isn't an accident.

No one gets hit.

But the man who watches smiles as his girlfriend says she wants to tell us something.

"Do you want to know," she says, grinning at him and at Rachel, "why he calls me Girl on Tongue?"

"Why?" I ask, wanting to know even though the couple are heavily tattooed and I'm holding Rachel's hand, hard.

"Come closer," the woman says. "I want to show you why my boyfriend calls me Girl on Tongue."

"Girl on Tongue?"

"Yes." She smiles at him, then at me.

"Why?" I ask.

"Yah," Rachel says. "Why?"

He strokes her arm, gently, tracing her tattoo sleeve with ring-jeweled fingers.

She opens her mouth for me, slowly. Very wide. Grabbing my elbows, she pulls me closer to her, my face to her open mouth, her tongue sticking out as she tries not to laugh and Rachel lets go of my hand.

I step closer, closer to her tongue. The woman wiggles it. I cringe. It's so long and flicking, as if dancing. In the very back of her mouth, the back of the tongue, it's a dark cavern of cavity-eaten teeth.

Her boyfriend steps behind me, puts his mouth near my ear and whispers, "She feels good enough about herself to admit her limitations."

I shiver, still gazing into her mouth. Her breath smells of chocolate mint, like Rachel's.

"When a woman finds courage to realize she's exactly the way she is, she discovers one of the true natures of her journey. She can detach herself from the whims of the ego and touch the deeper sources of her life, like Girl on Tongue." He smiles at me. "Go ahead. Touch it," he says, and I do.

Becoming real, open, vulnerable, receptive to a true spiritual awakening, I feel as if I'm falling into her mouth, deep, deep inside her as I leave with them, leaving Rachel behind.

Twenty years have passed, and I can barely recall Rachel's face.

GIRL IN CLOUD[214]

RAIN, AND THE SAME SKULL-WHITE CLOUDS[215] clouding over, tightening around me, squeezing me, spitting me out drop by drop.[216] Something about the rain, he says.[217] When it rains, locks click.[218] I'm alone for days.[219] Bucket to pee in and piles of candy, bottled water, magazines. Something about the rain would ruin me,[220] he says, so when clouds gather the hairs on

---

[214] When it rains, her captor smokes a hookah and she stares through smoke, a cloud.

[215] Behind the cloud of hookah smoke are skulls inside crumbling walls, remains of girls who were in the cloud before her.

[216] Rain dampens the walls, the makeshift room built around skulls so that the walls start to disintegrate in the damp hookah cloud.

[217] He can't quit talking about rain, afraid the walls will rot and fall through the water locks.

[218] A water lock is an enclosed, rectangular chamber with gates at each end. Water is raised or lowered to allow captive girls to overcome differences in water level as the basement floods. These water locks were sold as black-market antiques, stolen from the Panama Canal. Clicking open and closed in the rain, they are a game of staircase locks. The girl never knows when a lock will open onto another cloud. The smoke changes flavor from cherry to vanilla to apple to grape to chocolate to mocha or honeydew, but each cloud contains a different hookah-smoking captor.

[219] Hookah smoking is typically done in groups, with the same mouthpiece passed from person to person, until the cloud dissipates like mist over a river with old water locks.

[220] Babies born to hookah smokers are at increased risk for respiratory diseases.

my neck stand up.[221] I know he'll rush out and shove me back into the cloud he made to protect me from rain.[222]

---

[221] She keeps looking at the walls. She doesn't want to. But like the other girls who have gone into the walls after staring through the clouds, she can't help herself.
[222] Hookah is also called *narghile, argileh, shisha, hubble-bubble,* and *goza.* These are the names he has given each of the girls who have lived in his clouds. This girl is Goza. The ones in the wall are Shisha, Argileh, and Narghile. Hubble-Bubble is waiting in the glass case, where the clouds can't reach her.

GIRLS IN WINDOWS

THE GIRL IN YOUR BED[223] isn't in your bed. She stands on one leg[224] while she steps into her skirt.[225] Slides her skirt up her thighs,[226] around her waist. Glances at you as you glance at her.[227]

The girl in your bed stands facing the window,[228] blinds pulled tight, like your lips when I look.[229] You're still in bed, uncovered by covers.[230] The girl in your bed was supposed to be me.[231]

Like a girl in a movie poster,[232] she faints in the arms of her naked lover,[233] realizing they'll never become fine art.

---

[223] Engage the senses: spice rack, bubble bath, Prosecco dried in corn-silk hair.

[224] Pink flamingo posing near lily pad.

[225] Do I look too much?

[226] Skin sticky from Prosecco baptism in true Italian white made with Glera grapes: *spumante, frizzante,* or *tranquillo,* depending on the *perlage.*

[227] After the ordeal of removing her G-string with your teeth, putting on her face in the dark.

[228] Staring, she doesn't say anything, but body language.

[229] Maybe at your hands, at nothing. Maybe thinking of where your hands have been?

[230] Naked girls are jogging in the dark, laughing around sorority houses, long ponytails bouncing while boys in man buns do the elephant walk near fraternity houses' lighted windows.

[231] Things are a little crazy, but that's what girls do.

[232] *The Girl in Apartment 3B*

[233] *Sweat Stained Summer Shame*

They will be thrown away, recycled with newspapers, considered cheap[234] and low grade.

She tells herself there's nothing degrading about it, being in a movie poster,[235] paying her dues in Hollywood.

In Hollywood, she will go out of style quickly,[236] though her nude lover seems to never age.

Another up-and-comer, a young actress, is clamoring to play a younger version of her.[237]

Her lover's eyes drifting toward the younger actress, his arms slowly releasing her.[238]

As she senses him letting go, she's trapped inside a vanishing image of herself,[239] diminished, like a male author responding to a young woman questioning his brilliance.[240]

I rest my head on her legs.[241]

We're all wearing short black dresses with sheer stockings and black high heels.[242]

Blue eyes to brown eyes, she's shivering and pushing me to the girl on the bed, the girl on the balcony.[243]

I smile at the metrosexual[244] clinging to the emasculating harpy.

---

[234] *Spray Tan Secrets: The Sequel*

[235] *Pie Crust of the Heart*

[236] *Typewriters and Toolboxes*

[237] *Don't Tell Mama*

[238] *A Daughter's Revenge*

[239] *Chocolate and Chokeholds*

[240] *Love Among the Stacks: The Prequel*

[241] And smile at the camera hidden in the smoke detector.

[242] We're all starved thin as sticks, fake boobs just another sign of starvation.

[243] I actually like the girl on the balcony. I mean, I wish we could just hang out and watch TV.

[244] Meaning: his sexuality revolves around the Metro bus. He sits in the back and touches himself every time the bus stops for someone carrying a shopping bag.

144

We are their guests, prisoners[245] who must abide by the harpy's dress code.

Night in Harpy Hotel[246] is so long that there is a moment when I think she could never really love me,[247] but she turns around in her backless dress and I see the ink on her back.

I'm tattooed on her body,[248] just another girl in a black dress.

---

[245] By choice! I would never do anything I didn't want to do and I want to do all of it!

[246] Not an actual hotel.

[247] Meaning: go down on me when Metro's not around.

[248] Right next to her brother's name and her first dog's paw print.

GIRL IN JANE'S DESK

She wears a dress made of rice paper, using a damp teabag for a pillow, a withered cocktail napkin for a blanket.

GIRL IN TOWER

SWIPE LEFT, RIGHT, LEFT, RIGHT. Faces turn into texts, turn into Hey baby and salt on a glass. Morning after photos of lattes, foam swirled into a bird perched on a skull. Photos of me, taken while I was sleeping and did not consent. Photos of us eating dinner and smiling, posted on Facebook while I'm in the bathroom trying to escape through the fire door. Photos of some museum we didn't go to, photos of sunsets sent on accident because he's dating so many of us at once. Photos of somebody else's mom, so I know he can access stock photos. Photos of stop signs, because he's done. But no! Surprise! He works as an urban planner and he choreographed all of the stop signs on the avenue, wow! That's amazing, I say. I say That's amazing a lot. I also say That's interesting and Yes and Great. I say Of course, because of course, and I will, because I will and do. I do all of the ordinary things and some weird stuff, too. The weird stuff is always less interesting than the ordinary things and usually less surprising but more sexual but less frequently pleasurable. I say Just a minute when I mean Give me a fucking break. I grow my hair, grow it longer and longer, even when he suspects something's up with that hair.

I grow my hair because it's a silent activity. I grow my hair because he can't tell me not to. Hair is just hair, and it grows unless you cut it. It just goes on, like the stories he tells, like my excuses, my lateness, my car lights crashing through darkness on my way to another hotel. I've never seen his place. He lives in a tower. This is what he tells me: a tower. Forty-five stories and he's on top. Penthouse, with a private elevator. He flashes the key, which looks like the key to my diary in seventh grade. Pink or fuchsia, something bloody. It's just called The Tower. The doorman calls him Sir or Mister, but the doorman keeps changing, patchwork of light and other lives. He keeps me in hotels, feeds me in restaurants because he's not ready, he says, to take me home.

I say I don't mind. I say Home is where I lay my head. I say Home is where you are, SirDarlingMister. I say Ohhhh baby it feels so good. I say Can you slow down but he's already asleep. I look up at the light, which is always the same: flickering.

I say Room Service and Keep the change.

One day I toss the key in the air, the bloody key, and catch it in my palm, scratch on my skin that vanishes as it heals.

Why won't you bring me home, I say, pouting my special pout, the one he can't resist. Usually he lies, says something about renovations, elevator music, security cameras, secret service. This time he tells the truth, heft and weight of something real, stumbling over the simple word: wife.

There's another woman in the tower, staring over the city from the penthouse to each backlit room, dioramas of want and need. So many curtains parted, hotel rooms crackling with lives she can't read.

***

The first time I meet his wife in the tower I explain to her how I first came to understand women. I tell her my aged lover taught me about my own body when I was a young girl, craving knowledge and tenderness. Ever elegant, my lover was practiced. Approaching every act with extreme patience and kindness, even in the heat of passion, she stroked my hair in the evening light fading behind delicate curtains that smelled of rosewater. Because people had a way of talking, I understood love's anatomy was as brutally honest as my stolen diary, revealing our intimate acts in explicit detail but having no words for the gentle way she touched me.

***

There is a memory of her inside me and that memory is you, guiding me, telling me what to do. By the time you tell me to show his wife the way you touched me, she whispers he never loved her, not that way.

We order pink champagne and wait for his knock on the door.

As usual, you're wearing your sunglasses, because of light glancing off walls of glass, many stories high, touching the sun in his glass tower.

You keep whispering, but his wife doesn't know. She doesn't suspect you're kissing me in designer sunglasses while sipping pink champagne as we undress near the fireplace, the warmth of flames pleasant on our bodies as you whisper, *Don't take off your sunglasses.*

Icy bubbles burst over our tongues, as we savor unquenchable thirst, emboldened by the knowledge women vanish into taxi cabs, fragrant faces sheltered behind long hair.

We kiss each other slowly, faces deliciously hidden beneath curtains of silky strands, softly brushed.

Drinking pink champagne, spilling on pillows and laughing, we shake the bed.

I'm surprised to see strangers on balconies. Watching us, they're bathed in sunset, dusk etching pink-champagne sky.

I'm afraid of the strangers, shy as they watch, until I realize he is among them.

Backing against a wall, sliding into a corner, I try to hide.

Whimpering, I collapse.

Finally, you remove my sunglasses.

Closing my eyes, I cover my face with my hands. Huddling, crouching, I feel your hands gripping my elbows before turning me into her.

You're leading me about the room, pausing for her fingers to dance all over my body, playing spider legs over my arms, thighs, and belly. Moving with the lightest touch possible, her fingertips travel hollows of my back, my throat, and finally my face, encouraging me to finally open my eyes. When I do, I see I'm on display, facing him in his tower windows, wanting it all to end, until you say, *I love you.*

GIRL IN TROUBLE

THE POLICE DON'T BELIEVE ME NOW because

When I say there was a road back there in the woods where people would party, the officers say it was impossible to

It was all words, but

Off-roading, you could

A lot of trails back there became

Once the hunter targeted you, the only way to survive was

Hands reaching through windows at night, but

Hands grabbing me and other girls and women, pulling us from our houses, even though

Some women vanished in mid-sentence when these hands

Some vanished as

Some were taken while vacuuming, watching television, or

There were people who wore masks made of

Pantyhose, carpet, and torn shirts could be used as weapons if

There were certain rumors about a thing called a "death kit" that was just

When you were running through the woods and fell onto the trunk of a fallen tree, the tree wasn't a tree at all but a man dressed in camouflage, and when you fell on him,

Now the police tell me the man is

They say there's nothing they can do because

One officer said it was my fault, what happened to me,
since

He said I should be more careful the next time I decide to

He said a girl in trouble is like

She is her own worst enemy, unless

Maybe I should thank the police for teaching me that

But every time I think of thanking them, they

GIRL IN RANSOM NOTE

WE HAVE HER AND HAVE NOT SOLD HER YET, but will sell her at the drop of a hat. If you want her back, do as we say. She's not harmed, not damaged goods, but your inability to follow instructions could damage her beyond anyone's wildest imaginations. We have done much research about you, about her and you, and we know you would never harm her or make the mistake of talking to the police about what has happened. You already know enough about what has gone on in your own house.

We have arranged this carefully. If you fail to follow instructions, she dies. The police will automatically assume you are the murderer, as the case we've created against you will be airtight, proven by DNA, blood spatter, and fingerprints, already collected and ready to be planted and set in motion before decay sets in.

Please do not make us cut her fingers off to prove to you her toes, or even her hair, are out of the question.

Do not ask to speak to her. How dumb do you think we are?

Do not expect any photographs or for us to in any way prove she is alive. How stupid do you think we are? Besides, photographs can be faked.

Remember, if you want to ever see her again, we are in

charge. We are the only ones allowed to ask questions, make requests or demands.

Now is the time to trust us. Totally. Completely.

We are now your new God, if you want us to save her.

Have faith in us and believe. She will be fine, only if you follow our instructions to the letter. Without question.

Here are our requests, which you should do immediately, without asking why we want these things done. Don't think. Just do. And do fast. If you follow these instructions and do what we ask, we will know. If you deviate from our instructions, we will know.

Our instructions, henceforth known as "The Ten Commandments," are as follows:

1.) Go to that place in your garage, the stash of old gym equipment draped in spider webs. Crawl under the trampoline to locate the big spider web where one dragonfly has been captured. Without damaging the dragonfly, remove it from the web and put it in a clear clean jar, secured by a lid with icepick air holes. If the dragonfly is still alive, capture the spider and put it in the jar with the dragonfly, but whatever you do, don't damage the web.

2.) Collect the used tissues stashed in her bedroom, under the bed and in her underwear drawer. All of them. Leave none behind. (Note: Under her bed and in her underwear drawer are the obvious places. There are other places for you to find. Try to think as she thought—as she thinks. Think of her. Think of her alive, still thinking.)

3.) Inside your next-door neighbor's tackle box, in the top drawer, get the razor blade—not the new one, but the old rusted one—and use it to carve her initials into the least obvious tree in the park she liked best. If she didn't like one park more than the others, or if you never took her to the park, or if the park has since been paved, carve her initials into your next-door neighbor's garden shed, above the lawn mower.

4.) Amid old perfume bottles in your neighbor's master bathroom, on the mirrored tray, is a hairbrush full of hair. Remove this hair and commingle it with yours in the hairbrush at home.

5.) Call your neighbor every night at 6 o'clock. Hang up if they answer. Do not leave a message.

6.) Buy a birthday cake, her favorite kind: red velvet. Prop up the cake so there's space underneath. Carve a hollow core into the cake from below, so the surface, with her name in frosting, stays intact. Then fill the core with wrapping paper, as if you're confused, prone to mistakes, likely to damage what matters most.

7.) Ask to babysit your friend's children. Return them late.

8.) Practice speaking in the present tense, even when you have your doubts, even when things happened in the past, and they did, things happened years ago. Practice speaking of these things as if they are happening now.

9.) Leave us the money we requested. This is ransom, after all. Leave us money this way: one dollar bill, new, not wrinkled or torn or stained or damaged. Leave one dollar bill in a standard white envelope in your mailbox every two hours between 8 a.m. and 8 p.m. every day except Sunday. When you leave the envelope in your mailbox, raise the red flag. Keep your curtains closed at all times so that you never accidentally see the courier tasked with collecting the money. Do this until we tell you to stop.

10). If you figure out who we are (even on accident, even if it's not your fault, even if it's the most unlikely scenario, a series of coincidences and bad luck all around), turn yourself in immediately and accept your punishment. If you think you've figured out who we are but you aren't sure, casually approach the person or people you think we are and say, in a calm voice, "Hey fuckwad, are you the one ruining my life?" If it's us, we will respond calmly as well, and escort you to the police station, where your ransom begins.

GIRL INDEX

Girl in Pussy Bow
Girl in Pantsuit
Girl in PTSD
Girl in Rape Fantasy
Girl in Bondage
Girl in Stirrups
Girl in IV
Girl in CV
Girl in Escape Tunnel
Girl in Rehab
Girl in Therapy
Girl in Group Therapy
Girl in Support Group
Girl in Support House
Girl in Traction
Girl in Tampon
Girl in Tabloid
Girl in Scholarly Research
Girl in Glass House
Girl in Glass Ceiling
Girl in Proscenium
Girl in Scrim

Girl in Bathroom

Girl in Ditch

Girl in Wilderness

Girl in Abandoned House

Girl in Gingerbread House

Girl in House Proud

Girl in Apron

Girl in Porn Ring

Girl in G-String

Girl in Pasties

Girl in Blackmail

Girl in Love Triangle

Girl in Triangulation

Girl in Asphyxiation

Girl in Trauma Reenactment

Girl in Victim Impact Statement

Girl in Parole Hearing

Girl in Investigation

Girl in Evidence

Girl in Ribbons

Girl in Handcuffs

Girl in Backseat

Girl in Hot Seat

Girl in Hot Pants

Girl in Badlands

Girl in White Space

Girl in Whiteout

Girl in Stakeout

Girl in Police Shooting

Girl in Racial Profiling

Girl in Redistricting

Girl in Clinic Bombing

Girl in Anonymous Hotline

Girl in Grooming

Girl in Green Room

Girl in Full Moon

Girl in Cold Feet

Girl in Concrete

Girl in Clean Sweep

Girl in Police Interview

Girl in Wiretap

Girl in Tap Dance

Girl in Lap Dance

Girl in Peep Show

Girl in No-Show

Girl in Snowdrift

Girl in Tracks

Girl in Needle

Girl in Haystack

Girl in Halo

Girl in See-Through

Girl in Seashell

Girl in Half Shell

Girl in Well

Girl in Dumpster

Girl in Murder Investigation

Girl in Conspiracy Plot

Girl in Kidnap Ring

Girl in Girl Zoo Bust

Girl in Zoo Stripes

Girl in Aviary

Girl in Solitary

Girl in Theory

Girl in Survival Guilt

Girl in Court

Girl in Line Up

Girl in Thumbs Up

Girl in Hope

Girl in Release

Girl in Hiding

Girl in Revenge Plot

Girl in Recovered Memory

Girl in Tell-All Memoir

Girl in *Lifetime TV*

Girl in *Dateline NBC*

Girl in Lurid Exposé

Girl in *To Catch a Predator* Special Episode

Girl in *Cold Case File*

Girl in Miraculous Recovery

Girl in Safekeeping

~~Girl in Hotel Room~~

Girl in Hotel Room Under a False Name with Two Armed
    Guards Outside Her Door

Girl in Family Reunion

Girl in Family Reunification

Girl in Animal-Assisted Therapy

Girl in False ID

Girl in Real ID

Girl in Witness

Girl in Egress

Girl in Life Vest

Girl in Tunnel Vision

Girl in Cult Phenomena

Girl in Shotgun

Girl in Girl Zoo Reunion, 25th Anniversary

Girl in Direct-to-Video Documentary

Girl in Dungeon Recreation

Girl in Captor Interview

Girl in *60 Minutes*

Girl in Paparazzi Photos

Girl in Vigilante Justice

Girl in Private Investigation to Recover Remaining Girls

Girl in Psychological Evaluation

Girl in Trauma Ward

Girl in Love Nest

Girl in Love

ACKNOWLEDGMENTS

AIMEE AND CAROL WOULD LIKE TO THANK their family and friends for love and support and to acknowledge each other's friendship and shared vision in the making of this book, which is dedicated to our mothers and grandmothers.

Grateful acknowledgement is also made to the following publications in which selections from this book have appeared, sometimes in slightly different form or under different titles:

Bennington Review ("Girl in Pictures" and "Girl in Refrigerator")

The Coachella Review ("Girl in One-Act Play" as "The Incident")

Diagram ("Girl in Cloud")

Fiction International ("Girl in Medical Trials")

Fiction Southeast ("Girl in Doubt")

Glassworks ("Girl in Finger Web")

Gone Lawn ("Girl in Bunk")

Grub Street ("Girl in Lighthouse")

Hotel Amerika ("Girl in Library" as "Centerfold")

The Laurel Review ("Girl in Mansion," "Girl in Special Collector's Edition," and "Girl in Your Car")

Monkeybicycle ("Girl in Glass" and "Girls in Windows")

Necessary Fiction ("Girl in Knots")

New Delta Review ("Girl in Dog House")

The Normal School ("Girl in Atrophy" and "Girl in the Silent Room")

New Flash Fiction Review ("Girls in Bars")

Quarterly West ("Girl in Clock")

Salt Hill ("Girl in Cavity," "Girl in Centerfold," "Girl in Halfway House," "Girl in Jane's Desk," "Girl in the Mall," "Girl in Rape Kit," "Girl in Zoo," and "Girl on Tongue" as "Lost Girls")

Western Humanities Review ("Girl in Ransom Note," "Girl in Whitewashed World," and "Girl in Woman")

Winter Tangerine ("Girl in Drain")